LUCAS

BAYOU BROTHERHOOD PROTECTORS
BOOK THREE

ELLE JAMES

TWISTED PAGE INC

© 2024 Twisted Page Inc. All rights reserved.

ISBN EBOOK: 978-1-62695-520-2

ISBN PRINT: 978-1-62695-521-9

AUTHOR'S NOTE

Enjoy other military books by Elle James

Bayou Brotherhood Protectors
Remy (#1)
Gerard (#2)
Lucas (#3)
Beau (#4)
Rafael (#5)
Valentin (#6)
Landry (#7)
Simon (#8)
Maurice (#9)
Jacques (#10)

Visit ellejames.com for more titles and release dates
Join her newsletter at
https://ellejames.com/contact/

LUCAS

BAYOU BROTHERHOOD PROTECTORS
BOOK #3

New York Times & *USA Today*
Bestselling Author

ELLE JAMES

CHAPTER 1

"DANNY, we're gonna need more beer over here," Bernadette "Bernie" Bellamy waved at their friend and favorite waitress at the Crawdad Hole Bar and Grill.

Felina Faivre slid lower in her chair, her cheeks burning. "I haven't finished the beer I have. It's not that big a deal. Really."

Too late. Danielle French, the feisty little red-haired dynamo everyone referred to as Danny, hurried over and rested her empty serving tray on one hip and her fist on the other. "Who is he? What's he done? Do I need to stomp on his hairy ass to get his attention?"

Bernie nodded. "I'm all for it, but Felina has decided to take the high road."

Danny frowned. "Who are we talking about? New

guy or Marty the rat bastard who dumped you for your best friend?"

"Shh." Bernie pressed a finger to her lip. "Marty asked Trish to marry him," she whispered.

Danny's eyes widened. "Has it even been two weeks since he dumped you?"

Felina grabbed Danny's arm. "Please. It's not that big a deal."

"The hell it isn't," Danny said, her voice growing louder. "No one treats our favorite flower girl like gator excrement and gets away without some form of retribution."

Felina grimaced. "I appreciate your loyalty, but I'm really okay. We were drifting apart anyway. I should've seen it coming, but I was too busy with my shop to pay attention to our relationship."

"Meanwhile, he was screwing your best friend," Bernie pointed out. "For him to pop the question to Trish, they had to be going at it for longer than you two have been broken up."

"No shit, Sherlock," Danny said. "Want me to get Gisele to conjure up a Voodoo potion to give the jerk a massive case of jock itch?"

"Did I hear my name?" Gisele Gautier, the granddaughter of the local Voodoo Queen, sailed up to the table and slid into the seat on the other side of Bernie. She grinned. "Who are we plotting against? I love brewing up a little retribution."

"No, guys." Felina shook her head. "I don't need

4

vengeance. I need ideas on how to make it through the wedding without looking pathetic."

"What wedding?" Gisele asked.

"Marty asked Trish to marry him," Bernie filled Gisele in.

Gisele let out a low whistle. "Seriously? So soon?"

Felina's gut twisted at the reminder. She and Marty had been a couple since high school. Everyone in Bayou Mambaloa had expected them to get married, even Felina. She'd thought he was waiting to propose until he'd established himself as a successful insurance agent and she'd gotten her flower shop business solvent enough to hire another person to help. They'd both met their career goals, and he'd still not asked her to marry him.

Felina felt like she'd somehow failed at their relationship. She'd failed to see the truth. Marty hadn't asked her to marry him because of career timing. He hadn't wanted to marry her, period.

Gisele reached across the table and covered Felina's hand. "Do you want me to turn Marty into a frog?"

Felina gave a shaky laugh. "No, I don't." She squeezed her friend's hand. "I'm actually happy for Marty and Trish and wish them all the luck."

Danny snorted. "Trish will need all the luck. If he could dump you for her, who's to say he won't do that to Trish?"

"I can't think that way," Felina said. "Trish is my best friend."

Gisele's eyes widened. "Still?"

Danny frowned. "She stole your man. How can you still call her a friend?"

"She didn't steal him," Felina said.

"Did I hear you say someone stole something?" a feminine voice sounded behind Felina.

She turned to smile weakly at Shelby Taylor. "Nothing important."

"Only her boyfriend's heart," Danny said.

"Are you off duty tonight?" Felina asked, trying to steer the conversation away from her problem.

Deputy Shelby Taylor wore jeans and a white blouse instead of her uniform. "I'm on days this week. I'm meeting Remy here for dinner." She pulled up a chair and dropped onto it. "What did I miss?"

Felina closed her eyes, knowing the others would bring Shelby up to date on her dilemma.

"Trish stole Marty from Felina," Danny said.

"And now, they're getting married," Gisele added.

"She didn't steal him from me," Felina argued. "Apparently, I never owned his heart. He fell in love with Trish. I can't fault him for that. She's beautiful and nice."

"And duplicitous and not your friend if she was having an affair with Marty behind your back." Gisele's lips pressed together.

"You're too kind," Shelby said. "I'd dump her ass."

Felina shook her head. "I can't. I'm the only florist in Bayou Mambaloa."

All four women stared at her as if she'd lost her mind.

"Please, don't tell us you're going to do the flowers for their wedding," Danny said, shaking her head.

Felina grimaced. "I promised Trish I would."

"Forget the beer," Bernie said. "Bring the whiskey."

Danny marched to the bar, reached over the counter, grabbed a bottle of whiskey and four glasses, plunked them on her tray and hurried back, calling over her shoulder, "I'm taking my break. Don't bother me for fifteen minutes."

"Ladies," Felina said. "I don't want this to get blown out of proportion. I'm really okay with all of it."

"Obviously, you're not, or you wouldn't be at the Crawdad Hole on a Thursday night." Danny unscrewed the cap from the whiskey bottle and filled the five glasses. She handed one to Felina while Shelby, Bernie and Gisele snagged a glass for themselves. Danny sank into the seat beside Felina. "Here's to friends who don't screw your boyfriend."

"Hear! Hear!" Bernie, Shelby and Gisele chorused.

Felina's lips twisted. "I'll drink, but only because I know the whiskey's good. And, to be honest, I do need help."

"And you came to the right place." Danny drank

her glass of whiskey in one long gulp, then plunked the glass on the table. "So, what's it to be? Want me to put a hit out on Marty? I know a couple of coonasses who'd do it for a bottle of whiskey."

Shelby pressed her hands to her ears. "I did not just hear that."

"No," Felina said. "I just want ideas on..." she fought for the right words, "frankly, how to save face and get my mother off my back."

Bernie blinked. "Sweetie, you don't need to save face."

"She's right," Gisele agreed. "If anyone needs to save face, it's Trish and Marty."

"You know Bayou Mambaloa," Felina continued. "Everyone is feeling sorry for me. I'll be the biggest, most pathetic loser at Trish's wedding. If I had dumped Marty, it would be different. He dumped me; therefore, I'm the loser."

Gisele shook her head. "Felina, you have it all wrong. You're the winner. Marty didn't deserve you."

"She's right," Shelby said. "You dodged a major bullet."

"I know that," Felina said. "But my mother and the rest of our little gossipy town are feeling sorry for me. I don't want that. I need a plan to look strong, not weak."

"Then why did you agree to do the flowers for their wedding?" Gisele demanded.

"Yeah," Danny said. "You should've told them to shove it where the sun won't shine."

How did she get through to her well-meaning friends that she didn't want to come off as mad or vindictive? "I want to appear to be happy for them. But not in a pathetic way."

Shelby tapped her fingernail against the tabletop. "They need to think you've moved on to something better."

Bernie touched a finger to her chin. "You need to look like you dumped Marty for a better option." Her lips twitched and then stretched across her face. "You need a hunky wedding date."

Felina frowned. "I have to live in this town. How's that going to help when he only appears for the wedding and disappears afterward? I'll look like I can't keep a man."

Danny's eyes narrowed. "You could have your wedding date appear a couple of weeks before the wedding for the buildup."

"Then you could stage a breakup at the wedding. Only, you do the breaking up this time," Bernie offered.

"He'd have to be much better looking than Marty," Gisele noted.

"Absolutely," Bernie said.

"Nothing else will do," Shelby agreed.

Danny nodded. "And you have to have a go-to-hell dress that makes Marty regret dumping you."

"That's not necessary—" Felina started.

"Hell yes, it is," all four of her friends said at once.

Felina laughed. "Assuming I go along with this plan, where am I supposed to find a better-looking guy than Marty? He's one of the best-looking guys Bayou Mambaloa has to offer."

"True. Bayou Mambaloa doesn't have much to offer in the way of native men," Gisele said. "Besides, you need someone bulked up and maybe a little more dangerous looking."

As if conjured from Gisele's words, the door to the Crawdad Hole Bar and Grill opened, and ten men entered.

Each guy had broad shoulders and muscular arms. They looked like they could chew nails and spit them into boards.

"What about them?" Danny said.

Bernie grinned. "No kidding. Any one of them would be perfect, except my Gerard."

"And my Remy," Shelby added, raising a hand to her fiancé, Remy Montagne. "For that matter, you could hire one of them. Granted, the Brotherhood Protectors are more in the line of security or protective services than paid dates. They're all former special operations operatives with years of experience on the battlefield."

"Yeah, but could they handle the small-town battleground and the minefield of a wedding?" Gisele asked.

Bernie frowned. "Maybe some more than others. Wouldn't hurt to ask."

"I don't know..." Felina eyed the men, considering her friends' words. She wouldn't look so pathetic if she had one of these hunky men at her side for the next couple of weeks and as her date to the wedding.

Marty couldn't hold a candle to their flames. Especially the tall one with dark hair and bedroom eyes. She'd seen him around town. He'd even been into her shop on several occasions to purchase small vases of flowers. Probably for his girlfriend. Which meant he was completely out of the selection pool. He'd introduced himself as Lucas.

At that moment, Lucas looked her way and smiled.

Felina's heart fluttered, and a swarm of butterflies erupted in her belly. Holy hell. The man went from smoldering good looks to panty-melting-hottie with one stretch of his lips.

"It's a solid idea worth checking into," Shelby said as she pushed to her feet. "Do you want me to put a bug in Remy's ear and find out if someone would be willing to take the job?"

Heat filled Felina's cheeks. "No," she said quickly before Remy reached Shelby. "I want to think about it."

"Hey, beautiful." Remy stopped in front of Shelby, pulled her into his arms and kissed her soundly.

When he finally raised his head, he smiled down at her. "Miss me?"

"Mmm. A little. Remind me again why." She lifted her chin, and Remy kissed her again.

Felina's heart swelled for her friend. As a friend and a deputy sheriff, Shelby did so much for the people of Bayou Mambaloa. She deserved to be happy. And Remy made her happier than Felina could remember Shelby ever being.

What they had, the love they shared, was how it should be. Not the boring existence she'd had with Marty. She was glad he'd dumped her. It had saved her the trouble. However, since he'd left her, she'd been stopped on the street where neighbors and townspeople expressed their condolences and openly pitied her.

Some of her customers came to the shop just to tell her how sad they were that Marty had dumped her after all this time, leaving her unmarried and with no chance of finding a husband at her advanced age of thirty. If she waited too long, her eggs would dry up, and she'd never have children.

Her own mother was already setting her up with any unmarried man she could scrape up, determined to get a grandchild before she died. After all, Felina wasn't getting any younger.

"Guys," Danny said. "Get a room."

Shelby and Remy broke apart.

"Not a bad idea," Shelby said. "Do we have any food at home?"

"I think there's one slice of pizza left in the refrigerator," Remy said.

Shelby sighed. "It's enough for me, but you need more." She glanced at Felina. "Are you sure you don't want me to say anything?"

Felina's cheeks heated. "I'll figure out something."

Shelby shrugged. "I'm sure they could help."

God, she hated to think about all ten of the men knowing what a failure she was that she had to hire a date for a wedding. Maybe she'd take one of her mother's offerings. As soon as the thought surfaced, she squashed it. *Not in a million years.*

Why settle for weeds when you could have a bouquet of muscles?

No. She'd come up with some other way of deterring the gossips and appeasing her mother. Maybe she'd plan a vacation after the wedding, like an unhoneymoon to celebrate her near-miss.

Shelby and Remy moved toward a table where several of his friends had gathered.

Bernie stepped into Gerard Guidry's arms and tipped up her chin to receive his kiss. "Hey."

Felina swallowed hard on a groan. "I have to go."

"But you just got here," Danny said.

"And we haven't picked out your guy," Gisele added.

"I'm not convinced it's a good idea, and I need

some air." Felina tipped her head toward Bernie and Gerard.

"Oh." Danny's lips pressed together. "I get it. Misery loves company, not a reminder that some people are ecstatically happy." She rose from her chair. "I have to get back to work anyway. Do you want me to walk you out to your car?"

"No, I'll be fine. It's still early," Felina said.

"Never too early for the drunks to get stupid," Danny said with an arched brow.

"I've got my pepper spray." Felina pulled the small container from her purse.

"Yeah, well, keep your hand on it," Danny said.

"I will." Felina headed for the rear door.

The man called Lucas appeared in front of her. "You're not leaving, are you?"

Felina's heart skipped several beats. She shook her head. "No," she lied. "I need to visit the ladies' room."

"Oh, well, don't let me hold you up." He stepped to the side. "When you get back, I'd like to buy you a drink."

Felina scurried away, wondering if Shelby had spilled the beans to this hunkworthy man that her pathetic friend needed a man in her life—at least for a wedding she didn't want to attend.

Holy hell. Would the humiliation never cease?

She headed for the hallway leading toward the rear exit, passing the bathrooms on the way. She didn't slow until she pushed through the door into the balmy night air.

For a moment, she stood on the back landing, breathing deeply until her heartbeats slowed and she could think straight.

She was about to step off the landing when the back door slammed open, and she turned halfway around to see who it was.

A man rushed through so fast that he plowed into Felina, nearly knocking her off the stoop.

He wrapped his arms around her to keep them both from flying off the landing. "What the fuck," he muttered, teetering on the edge.

Headlights flashed at one end of the gravel parking lot.

The man's hand slid into her front jeans pocket.

"Don't touch me!" Felina demanded as she positioned her little can of pepper spray over her shoulder, hoping to get the man's eyes and not hers. She pressed the button.

The man yelled and pushed her so hard she flew off the stoop, landing on her hands and knees in the gravel, the pepper spray skidding out of reach.

She looked back at the man above her.

"Fuck!" The man swayed on the stoop, rubbing his eyes.

One more step in the wrong direction and he'd fall, landing on top of Felina.

He took that step.

Felina tucked and rolled back toward the stoop as the man tumbled off the landing.

He landed in a heap on the gravel in the spot she'd just vacated.

He staggered to his feet, his eyes tightly closed. "Bitch! I'm gonna kill you!"

Before Felina could rise to her feet and run, a black SUV with darkly tinted windows blew through the back alley and skidded to a stop in front of the man she'd pepper-sprayed.

A big man, wearing a dark suit and sunglasses, leaped out of the SUV, grabbed the man by the shoulders, shoved him into the back seat and climbed in beside him. The door slammed, and the SUV spun out of the parking lot.

Felina lay in the shadow of the stoop, waiting for the SUV to move far enough away to allow her to read the numbers and letters on the license plate. Unfortunately, there was no license plate.

The SUV disappeared around the corner of the building.

Felina pushed to her feet and stared down at her bloody hands and torn jeans.

The back door opened, and a man stepped out.

Felina tensed, ready to run.

The man's face was cast in shadow from the light shining down on the back of his head.

When he turned toward her, he murmured. "What the hell?"

Felina whirled to run. Before she could take two steps, the man flew off the stoop, landing in the gravel beside her.

He grabbed her arms and spun her around.

"Let go of me!" she yelled and pounded her fists against his chest.

"Felina, it's me, Lucas," he said in a low, rich tone. "It's okay. It's just me."

She stared up into the warm brown eyes of the man who'd bought multiple bouquets of flowers in her shop. When her mind registered him as a friend rather than an enemy, she sagged against him.

"Sweetheart," he said softly, "are you hurt?"

"Not much," she whispered.

He tipped her chin up and stared down into her eyes. "What the hell happened?"

CHAPTER 2

LUCAS HAD WAITED in the barroom, his gaze on the dimly lit hallway where the bathrooms were located. He was determined to buy the pretty florist a drink and hopefully get to know her better.

He'd purchased half a dozen flower arrangements at her shop, hoping to strike up a conversation with her, only to be greeted by her assistant each time. That tactic wasn't working. Finding her at the Crawdad Hole seemed a perfect opportunity to take his game to the next level.

A man in a black leather jacket sprang up from a chair in the corner with a cell phone pressed to his ear. He listened for a moment, then shoved the phone into his pocket and walked quickly toward the bathroom hallway.

Lucas's gut knotted. Something about the man's face didn't sit right with him. His expression was too intense for a man coming to a bar for a casual drink. The guy entered the hallway where Felina had gone a few moments earlier.

Lucas followed, concerned for Felina.

By the time Lucas entered the hallway, the man had broken into a run. He hit the back exit door hard, sending it crashing open. The man rushed out, and the door swung closed behind him.

Lucas started to follow but remembered Felina had gone to the latrine.

He paused in front of the ladies' restroom door and knocked. "Felina?"

A brunette opened the door. Not the pretty strawberry-blond florist he'd expected.

She stood in the doorframe and ran her gaze from the top of Lucas's head to the tips of his boots. "Mmm. I'm not Felina, but you can call me Felina, Deloris, Maggie or Jane. As long as you call me." She winked. "Want my number?"

Lucas shook his head and looked past her through the open door. "Felina?" he called out.

"I was the only one in there." She stepped past him. "If you change your mind about my number, I'll be at the bar."

Lucas backed away, spun and ran to the exit.

He pushed through the door and stepped out of the building. That was when he'd found Felina standing in the gravel parking lot, looking down at her hands.

Now, with her pressed close to his chest, Lucas's pulse pounded hard against his ribs. "What the hell happened?"

"That man..." she said.

"The one who left through the rear door before me?"

She nodded. "He grabbed me, felt me up and then shoved me hard. I fell off the step and landed in the gravel."

Anger ripped through Lucas. He glanced around, looking for the man. "Where did he go?"

Felina turned her head toward the corner of the building. "A dark SUV drove up, and a big man got out and pushed the man into the back seat. They went that way." She tilted her chin toward the side of the building. "I don't think he wanted to go with them. I tried to get a license plate number, but the SUV didn't have one."

Lucas wished he could get his hands on the man who'd roughed up the pretty florist. He leaned back and looked into her face, the light shining over the door glancing off her irises. "Are you hurt?"

She held out her hands, palms up. "Just some scrapes on my hands and knees where I landed."

"Let's get you inside where we can clean those wounds."

"I'm okay," she insisted, her body trembling.

"You're not okay." He slipped his arm around her

and guided her to the back door. When he tried the handle, it wouldn't open.

"It locks automatically," Felina explained. "You can leave through the back door but can't enter through it without a key."

"Then we'll go around the front."

"I really am okay." Her words said one thing. The fact she hadn't moved out of the curve of his arm gave an entirely different message.

Lucas wasn't turning her loose until he was absolutely sure she was okay. "Come on. I'll bet there's a first-aid kit behind the bar."

When he started to lead her around the side of the building, she planted her feet in the gravel. "I don't want to make a big fuss."

"And I don't want your hands to become infected." He turned her toward him and lifted those hands in his. "You work with your hands. Either let me dress the wounds or let me take you to an emergency room and have a doctor or nurse do the job."

"The nearest emergency room is thirty miles away. I can take care of myself at home."

"Then I'm going with you."

Her brow furrowed. "I barely know you."

"I'm a regular at your shop."

Her frown deepened. "What would your girlfriend say about you going to another woman's house?"

His brow twisted. "What girlfriend?"

21

One delicate eyebrow lifted. "The one you bought all those floral arrangements for."

His cheeks heated. "Those were for me." He wasn't about to tell her he'd only purchased them to get closer to her. She'd think he was some kind of stalker. "Can I help it if I like fresh flowers? If you're not comfortable with me going with you to your home, then let me or one of your friends help you here."

She sighed. "Fine. We'll go inside."

He grinned. "Good. And after we clean up your hands, I'll buy you that drink I promised."

"That's not necessary," she said, allowing him to lead her around the side of the building to the front.

"Just one," he urged. "I was really looking forward to trying out my best pickup lines."

"You need pickup lines?" She gave him a sideways glance.

He shrugged. "I've been out of the dating scene for a while. I'm out of practice." He opened the front door of the Crawdad Hole Bar and Grill and held it wide for her. "You'd be doing me a favor."

She snorted. "I've been out of the dating game for a while as well, and I have no intention of jumping back in. I'm not sure I'd be a good sounding board for your practice."

"Then you could give me an unbiased opinion," he said with a grin.

Her brow twisted. "First, let's see how good your

first aid skills are." As she stepped through the door, she stopped short. "I'd rather not stir up my friends.".

He glanced toward the women, who all looked toward them at once. "Too late. You have incoming."

The women moved as one toward Lucas and Felina.

Lucas's boss, Remy, and his teammate Gerard followed.

"Crap," Felina murmured. "Brace yourself, and don't let them talk you into anything."

"What do you mean?" he asked.

Before she could answer, the four women converged on them.

A petite, dark woman with raven-black curly hair and golden eyes reached them first. "So, he's the one, huh?"

"No," Felina said, trying to push through the women. "I took a tumble in the parking lot. He just happened to be there." She held up her hand. "Don't get any ideas."

"A tumble in the parking lot?" Remy's woman, Shelby, frowned. "Are you okay?"

"I'm fine," Felina said.

"She didn't just take a tumble," Lucas said. "A man pushed her off the back porch. Her hands and knees are scraped and need attention." With his hand at the small of Felina's back, he eased his way through her friends.

"I'll get the first-aid kit," the waitress, Danny, said.

"You can bring her back behind the bar to rinse her hands in the sink."

Danny led the way around to the back of the bar to the sink and turned on the water, adjusting the temperature.

The other women, Remy and Gerard slipped onto the barstools.

Lucas guided Felina's hands beneath the water.

She winced and pulled her hands back.

"They hurt, but they need to be cleaned," he said softly into her ear, his arms going around her to ease her palms beneath the faucet.

"Okay?" he asked.

She nodded.

He squirted liquid hand soap into her palm and lathered them gently. "Feel any grit or pieces of gravel embedded?"

She shook her head.

Danny draped a towel over Lucas's shoulder. "That's a freshly laundered towel. Do you want me to take over?"

"No, thank you," he said. "Unless that's what Felina wants."

"No. You're doing fine," she said.

"You say a man pushed her?" Remy asked.

Shelby leaned over the bar. "Did you recognize him?"

Felina shook her head. "I don't think he was from around here. I've never seen him before."

"Did he leave in a vehicle?" Shelby continued. "Did you get a license plate? I could run the plate."

Felina grimaced. "I looked, but the SUV he left in didn't have a plate on the back. And he didn't look all that happy about being shoved into the backseat."

"Make and model?" Shelby pulled out her cell phone and placed a call.

"Big, black, with tinted windows. That's all I got. I was on my hands and knees in the gravel when the SUV blew into the back parking lot. A big guy got out, grabbed the guy who shoved me and threw him into the backseat. They took off in a cloud of dust."

"I'll tell the department to be on the lookout for a big black SUV with no tags."

"Why?" Felina asked.

Lucas turned off the water and wrapped Felina's hands in the clean towel.

"You could file assault charges on him," Shelby said.

"He shoved me. I fell. It's not like he continued to assault me," Felina said.

"He shouldn't have shoved you in the first place," Shelby said.

"I was standing in his way on the landing when he burst through the door. It could've been an accident...him running into me."

"You said he felt you up before he shoved you," Lucas reminded her.

"He did what?" Shelby shook her head.

"He grabbed my hips and slipped his hands into my pockets. I was too shocked to say anything. And then he was shoving me forward."

Shelby lifted her cell phone to her ear and turned away to report the incident to the sheriff's department.

Lucas inspected her hands. "I think the bleeding has stopped. Do you want me to put bandages on the cuts?"

Felina shook her head.

"Now, let me look at your knees." He led her around to one of the barstools, grabbed her around the waist and lifted her onto the seat.

"I could have done that myself," she murmured.

"And put your clean hands with open wounds on a bar stool that who knows how many people have touched?" Lucas pressed his lips together. "Stay."

He went back to the bar sink, rinsed the clean towel beneath the faucet and squeezed out the excess water. When he returned to Felina, he dropped to a squat and examined her torn jeans. "Hold this," he said and handed her the damp towel. "It would be better if you could take off the jeans."

"Not an option," Felina said, her mouth crimping.

"I figured you'd say that." Lucas grinned and carefully rolled up her pants legs so that he could get to her scuffed knees. With care, he wiped away the blood and dirt. "Can someone hand me a large bandage?" He held out his hand.

Danny dug through the kit, unearthed a large adhesive bandage and handed it to him. "Need another?"

"A smaller one." He peeled the backing off the bandage and applied it to her left knee. "The abrasion isn't too bad, but I didn't want to roll the dirty jeans back over an open wound." He applied a smaller bandage to the opposite knee and rolled the pants legs down. He pushed to his feet. "I think you'll live."

Gerard stood beside his woman, Bernie. "Just like old times, performing self-care in the field."

Bernie grinned and turned to Shelby. "You thinking what I'm thinking?"

Shelby nodded. "I am."

"Me, too," Danny said, crossing her arms over her chest. "I think you have a winner."

Lucas looked from Danny to Felina. "What are they talking about?"

Felina's cheeks had flushed a rosy pink. "Nothing," she answered quickly. "You said you'd buy me a drink. I could use one about now."

"But Felina, you know he's perfect," the petite woman with the curly black hair said.

"Shhh." Felina gave a quick jerk of her head toward her friend. She smiled tightly at Lucas. "Maybe we could get a table where we could be alone."

"Felina—" Bernie started.

Danny reached out and grabbed the woman's arm. "Leave her alone. She's got this."

The four women exchanged a glance and nodded as one.

Danny pointed to an empty table in a dark corner of the bar, scattered with empty mugs and beer bottles. "Come on. I'll clear that table and get you two a drink."

Lucas wasn't sure what was going on. His gut told him he was the object of some conspiracy. But he was too thrilled to get Felina relatively alone to care.

As they waded through the tables, a woman burst through the entrance of the bar and called out, "Oh, Felina!"

Felina stiffened and turned toward the blonde, who quickly crossed the floor to stand in front of her. "Trish," Felina said with a curt nod.

"I'm so glad I ran into you." She glanced around the barroom, her gaze panning the patrons.

"Were you looking for me?" Felina asked.

"No," the blonde said, clearly distracted, as if searching for someone. "I was supposed to meet someone here, but I don't see him." Her attention returned to Felina. "But isn't this serendipitous? I had some ideas about the flowers for the wedding I wanted to run by you before you make the order."

Felina frowned. "Could it wait until morning? I'm a little busy right now."

"Oh," Trish looked from Felina to Lucas, her eyes

rounding. "Am I interrupting a date?" A grin spread across her face.

The color in Felina's cheeks deepened. "I—"

The woman called Trish clapped her hands. "See? I told Marty you'd find someone who suits you much better than him. He said you wouldn't."

Felina's lips pressed into a tight line. "He said that?"

Trish nodded, her blond hair bouncing. "How smart of you to find a man so soon. Will he be your plus one at the wedding?"

Felina lifted her chin, hooked her hand through Lucas's elbow and smiled at the blonde. "As a matter of fact, yes."

"Oh, good. I'm so relieved. I hated to think of you coming alone." The blonde leaned in and hugged Felina. "I'm so glad we're still friends. No hard feelings, right?" She straightened and looked around. "Now, I need to find the guy I was supposed to meet about a business matter. I'll drop by your shop tomorrow to discuss the flowers." She stepped away with a wiggle of her fingers. "Toodles!"

Felina stood for a moment longer, her body stiff.

"What was that all about?" Lucas asked.

"Nothing," she muttered and made a beeline for the table in the corner Danny was wiping with a rag.

The waitress straightened as Felina and Lucas approached. "Was that Trish?"

Felina nodded.

"Want me to punch her in the throat?" Danny looked over her shoulder toward the blonde moving around the barroom. "Or I could spit in her drink or spike it with flaming hot tabasco sauce."

Lucas blinked at the venom in Danny's tone.

"No, don't do that. Trish is just...Trish. And I might've said something that I didn't mean."

"You told her to go to hell and that you wouldn't do the flowers for her wedding?" Danny grinned.

"No. I told her Lucas would be my plus one at her wedding."

Danny's gaze went to Lucas. "Really? That's great." She shook his hand. "Thanks for taking care of our girl."

Lucas's head was spinning. He wasn't quite sure what had just happened, but he didn't let on to Felina's friend. "Anything for our girl," he murmured.

"Damn right." Danny's eyebrows dipped low. "Just don't hurt her, will you? She's already been through enough."

Lucas held up his hands. "I have no intention of hurting her."

"Good." Danny's eyes narrowed. "Because if you do, I'll find you and make you wish you hadn't done it." Her face cleared, and a smile softened her features. "There. Your table is ready. Can I get you a beer?"

Lucas nodded, hoping the waitress wouldn't spit in it or spike it with hot sauce.

After Danny left, Lucas held out a chair for Felina and waited for her to settle before dropping into the chair beside her. "Mind telling me what that was all about?"

Felina's brow puckered. "Wouldn't you rather practice your pickup lines?"

Lucas shook his head. "Not when I think I've just been volunteered to be a plus-one at a wedding for people I've never met."

Felina grimaced. "About that..." She drew in a deep breath.

Lucas straightened, his gut telling him to brace himself.

CHAPTER 3

FELINA STRUGGLED to find the words to explain to this handsome man why he'd just been tagged as her plus one without sounding pathetic. "I don't know where to begin."

"Start with the blonde," he said. "Trish, I think you said. Who is she, and why am I going to her wedding as your plus one?"

Squaring her shoulders, Felina lifted her chin. "Trish was—is my best friend. I'm doing the flowers for her wedding."

"Okay...and why did you feel the need to tell her I was your plus one?"

Felina winced. "She's marrying my ex-boyfriend." There. She'd said it.

Lucas nodded, his eyes narrowing. "Isn't there some unwritten female rule that friends don't poach on a friend's ex-boyfriend?"

Her lips pressed together. "He wasn't my ex-boyfriend at the time."

Lucas's eyes widened. "She was fooling around with your boyfriend while you were still together? And Trish is still your friend?"

"We told her she was a fool to still be friends with Trish." Danny plunked two mugs of beer on the table in front of them, then straightened. "She should've scratched her eyes out or at least slashed her tires."

Lucas winced. "Remind me not to get sideways with you."

"Don't screw with my friends, and we'll be good," Danny said. She looked at Felina. "You okay?"

Felina nodded. "I am."

"Look, if this guy doesn't want the job, we'll find someone else." Danny gave Lucas a stern glance. "If he knows what's good for him, he'll take the job." She pointed two fingers at her own eyes and then at Lucas. "I'm watching you."

Lucas held up his hands. "Hey, don't spit in my beer. I'm just an innocent bystander who happened to find your friend in the gravel out back."

"Yeah, but you're a man." Danny's mouth pressed into a tight line. "You can't trust men." A shout from a table nearby caught the waitress's attention. She hurried away, muttering beneath her breath, "Bellowing bastards can damn well wait."

Lucas's gaze followed Danny. "Is she always so scary?" He turned back to Felina.

Felina smiled. "She works here, doesn't she? You have to be a little badass to put up with some of the customers. We have all kinds coming out of the bayou for a drink." She smiled. "She had a bad breakup with a guy a couple of years back. Since then, she's put up a wall where men are concerned."

"It's damned effective," Lucas said. "And you?"

Her smile faded. "What?"

"The ex?" He tipped his head toward the blonde who'd slid onto a stool at the far end of the bar. "Was it a bad breakup?"

"A bit unexpected," Felina said. "I never knew he was seeing my best friend while we were supposedly still a couple."

Lucas took her hand. "Sounds like you dodged a bullet."

Felina's lips twisted. "Shelby said the same thing. What's with you gun-toting people and your bullet analogies?"

He grinned. "It's what we know."

"I guess." Her gaze was still on Trish, where she sat alone at the end of the bar. She'd said she'd come to meet someone about business. What business? Trish owned a beauty shop.

"Did you love him?" Lucas asked.

"What?" Felina yanked her thoughts back to the man holding her hand. She tugged her fingers free of his. "What was your question?"

His eyebrows rose. "Did you love him?"

34

Felina's eyes narrowed. "I thought I did. We'd been together since high school. Everyone expected us to marry someday. Then he broke up with me, and two weeks later, he was engaged to Trish."

"Two weeks?" Lucas shook his head. "How long had they been seeing each other behind your back?"

"I'm not sure." She met his gaze. "I should've seen it, though, but I was so busy with my shop, I guess I lost sight of what Marty was doing when he wasn't with me."

"Obviously, he was screwing around."

"Yeah. Which makes me look like a fool. Now, every gossiping neighbor in the parish feels obligated to tell me how sorry they are for me and to tell me it's not too late to find another man before my child-bearing days are over."

"Seriously?" Lucas shook his head.

Felina pressed her lips together. "No matter how many times I tell them I'm okay, they don't believe me. Some have even brought their sons or nephews to the shop for me to meet, hoping to find my perfect consolation prize for having lost out on marriage to Marty. Even my mother has been dragging potential suitors into my shop for me to consider. I can't take it anymore."

"That's tough," Lucas said. "I can't believe you're still talking to the other woman."

"I kind of have to." Felina looked away. "She asked

me to provide the flowers for their wedding in two weeks."

His eyebrows shot up his forehead. "And you said yes?"

"I'm the only florist in Bayou Mambaloa. If I had said no, I would appear churlish or worse...like I still have feelings for Marty."

"And do you?" Lucas asked softly.

She shrugged. "It's hard to shut off all feelings for someone you thought you'd marry. I do have feelings for him. But not the passionate, can't-live-without-you kind of feelings. More like a nostalgia for what was and no longer can be."

"Even though he dumped you for your best friend?" Lucas shook his head. "You're a lot more forgiving than I'd be."

"I feel a little at fault in this scenario," she said.

"How so? You didn't cheat on him, did you?"

"No. Nothing like that." She looked into Lucas's eyes. "Relationships take work. I didn't put any effort into ours. I think we were drifting apart even before he hooked up with Trish. If I'd felt strongly enough about us, I would've worked harder. I guess I didn't feel strongly enough."

"And the need for a plus one at the wedding has to do with the marriage-minded mamas looking to match you with their boys?"

She nodded. "They're driving me crazy. I just

need all of this to die down so I can focus on my business. I hope that once the wedding is over, they'll quit bothering me. Until then, my meddling neighbors will bring their boys to the shop, my mother will dig up some toothless Cajun to take me to the wedding, and I won't get a moment's rest." She crossed her arms and rested them on the table, leaning toward him. "Which brings me to you."

"Your plus one," he said with a twisted grin.

"I had been toying with the idea of hiring someone to pretend to be my boyfriend for the two weeks leading up to the wedding and then have him be my date for the big day." She narrowed her eyes. "Since I jumped the gun and kind of lied about you being my plus one, I'm in somewhat of a corner. You're one of those Brotherhood Protectors like Remy and Gerard, right?"

He nodded, his brow dipping low. "Yeah."

She continued. "You hire out for some kind of security service?"

"We do," he said.

"What if I hire you to protect me from all those well-meaning friends and relatives until I can get past this damned wedding?" She cringed. "I mean, it's not like being a bodyguard to a celebrity or politician, but I would pay good money. Would you be at all interested?"

Lucas tapped a finger to his chin and looked at

her consideringly. "As an agent with the Brotherhood Protectors and former Delta Force operator, I take my duties seriously."

"I understand," she sighed. "This would be beneath you." She reached across the table and grabbed his hands with both of hers and winced at the reminder that her injuries were still fresh and raw. "Look, I'm desperate. I need a break. My shop needs a break. I can't get any work done when I have to wade through the 'candidates' on a daily basis. Will you be my fake boyfriend for the next two weeks and go with me to a wedding I have no desire to attend?"

"I don't know..." Lucas said.

She glanced over his shoulder at the other members of his team gathered around a table, laughing and joking with each other. "If not you, do you think one of your teammates would consider the job? I mean, I could possibly get around the fact it isn't you..."

He laced his fingers with hers. "I'll do it," he said. "On one condition..."

Relief flooded through her. "Fine. Anything. What's the condition?" she asked.

"I take my work seriously. We have to make our fake relationship look real to convince others."

She nodded. "Obviously, or my mother will continue to look for other men to throw at me."

"We'll have to spend a lot of time together."

"That's a given," she agreed.

His gaze met and held hers. "There'll have to be PDA."

Felina frowned. "PDA?"

"Public displays of affection," he rolled his hand, "like kissing, holding hands, hugging."

Butterflies beat their wings against the insides of her belly. "Right."

"But sex is off limits," he said.

A sudden rush of heat pushed through her veins at the thought of making love with the former Delta Force soldier, followed by a strange stab of disappointment that it would never happen. "Without a doubt," she said. "I'm paying for security services, not...other services."

"Right." He held up a finger. "Unless..."

Something that felt oddly like hope dared to blossom inside Felina's chest. "Unless?" she said, her voice breathy.

"Unless it's mutually agreed upon."

"No worries," she said. "This is strictly a business arrangement."

"And you don't strike me as someone who mixes business with pleasure."

"Exactly." She drew in a shaky breath, wondering what she'd just agreed to, but couldn't back out now. "So, it's a deal?"

"It's a deal."

She held out her hand.

Lucas took her hand in his. "PDA starts now, and a handshake isn't going to convince anyone." His fingers curled around hers, his grip tightening.

Before she could guess his next move, he pulled her out of her chair and onto his lap.

"What are you doing?" she gasped.

"PDA." He cupped the back of her neck and claimed her mouth.

Shocked at the sudden move, Felina's mouth was open, allowing Lucas to sweep in and caress her tongue with his.

At first stiff, she eventually melted into him, automatically returning the kiss, her hands sliding around his neck and weaving into his thick, dark hair.

Felina was so caught up in that one kiss they could have been the only people in the entire barroom.

When they were forced to come up for air, she blinked her eyes, the room and the people in it coming into focus.

Danny glided past with a tray full of empty bottles. "I thought you said you didn't know each other."

"We don't," she whispered.

"Dude," a voice called out, "get a room."

Felina turned to see who was speaking.

She was appalled to find all of Lucas's teammates staring at them with grins on their faces.

"Yeah, man, get a room," another man said. "You're making the rest of us jealous."

"Not a bad idea." Lucas scooted Felina off his lap and onto her feet, then rose, taking her hand in his. "Y'all have a good evening," He gave them a mock salute. "Ready to go?" he asked Felina.

She nodded, her cheeks on fire, embarrassed at being the center of attention for the entire barroom.

"Hey, Lucas," someone shouted. "Does she have a sister?"

Lucas glared at the man. "Shut up, Sin. Even if she did, I wouldn't wish her on the likes of you."

The man Lucas had called Sin pressed a hand to his chest. "You wound me."

"Come on." Lucas leaned close to Felina. "Let's get out of here before they get any rowdier."

As they headed for the door, Gisele raced up to Felina. "You picked a good one. I hope it works out." She hugged her. At the same time, she shoved something into Felina's back pocket. "A little protection in case you need it." Then she stepped back, allowing them to pass through the door and into the parking lot.

Felina drew in a deep breath and let it out slowly. She hadn't realized just how keyed up she'd been until that moment. Acting like they were already lovers had been intense. And that fake kiss... Wow. That hadn't felt fake. Not on her part, anyway.

Now, alone with Lucas, Felina wasn't sure how to act. "Uh," she struggled for words. "Well, I guess it's good night."

He frowned. "Now that I'm your boyfriend, I need to see you safely to your door." He looked around. "Where's your car?"

"Actually, I rode with Bernie. But it's not far to my shop. I can walk."

"That's over a mile." Lucas shook his head. "There's no way a boyfriend would let his gal walk home in the dark." He took her hand. "I'll drive you."

She gave a halfhearted attempt at pulling her hand free. "That's not necessary. There are plenty of streetlights to light my way."

"After that guy pushed you down and was shoved into a vehicle and whisked away...? I don't feel comfortable letting my teammates walk home alone, much less my girlfriend." Lucas grinned.

"Still…" she started, "I don't want to take advantage of your services."

Lucas stood still, holding her hand. "If we're going to make this look real, you need to let me act like a real boyfriend. Besides, my job is to have your six, whether it's to keep the meddling mamas from shoving potential grooms in your face or to keep would-be attackers from taking advantage of a lone female walking across town at night. I'm your man. If you're afraid I'll push the limits, don't worry." He held up his hand like a Boy Scout. "I promise to see you to your door and no further."

Felina was a little intrigued by the push-the-limits phrase and possibly a little disappointed he wasn't going to even try. "Okay. I would appreciate a ride home. I've been on my feet all day in the shop. It would be nice not to have to walk that mile."

He looped her arm through the crook of his elbow and marched her to a giant four-wheel-drive pickup.

She blinked up at it. "This is yours?"

He nodded. "It is. When we heard we would be based out of the bayous of Louisiana, I figured a four-wheel drive might come in handy. I don't want to get stuck in the mud, and it has a winch in case I do."

She stared at the door, high above her. "I'll need a ladder to get up into that thing."

He chuckled, reached for the door handle and opened the passenger door. A running board dropped down, providing a convenient step that would allow her to climb up into the truck.

"That's handy," she commented and reached up into the truck for a handhold.

Lucas grasped her around the waist and assisted her up into the passenger seat. "Need help with the seatbelt?"

She shook her head, her heart beating fast and her

breaths coming in shallow gasps. His hands around her waist had been large, warm and strong. Her immediate thought had been of those hands smoothing across her naked skin, cupping her breasts.

Get a grip, girl, she chastised herself. He's a paid security guard, not a paid escort or gigolo, and this was a legitimate business arrangement that wouldn't last more than two weeks. Then they'd part ways and never see each other again.

Except he would still be in Bayou Mambaloa between security gigs. She'd bump into him on occasion. All the more reason to keep their interactions platonic, except for a few kisses and... What had he called it? Oh, yeah. PDA. They wouldn't convince anyone they were an item unless they did some hugging, hand-holding and kissing in public.

Lucas rounded the front of the massive truck, climbed effortlessly into the driver's seat and started the engine.

Felina didn't have to give him the address. He'd been there on several occasions in the past few weeks, ordering flowers.

The drive to her shop didn't take long, making Felina all the happier she'd agreed to let Lucas drive her there. It would have taken a lot longer to walk the short distance. And, though she wouldn't admit it to the Delta, she was a little spooked by the man who'd thrown the other man into the backseat of the

SUV. She wondered what had happened to the one who'd pushed her. Had they taken him to rough him up or kill him?

She shivered at the thought and made a mental note to touch base with Shelby the following day to see if the sheriff's department had located the SUV without a license plate.

As Lucas pulled to a stop in front of the flower shop, Felina unbuckled her seatbelt. "Thank you for the ride," she said, her hand on the door handle.

"My pleasure," he said as he shoved open the door and dropped to the ground.

Felina shoved open the heavy door and slipped out of her seat, her feet feeling for the running board.

Before she could get her footing, those strong hands gripped her waist again.

Lucas lifted her out of the truck.

She wrapped her arms around his neck to stabilize herself and then slid down his front, landing on her feet.

At that point, he didn't immediately release her.

He pressed a kiss to her forehead and whispered, "Do you have nosey neighbors around your shop?"

"Just the widow who lives above the real estate office across the street." Her back was to Mrs. Lebowitz's upstairs apartment. "Is the light shining around the curtains?" she asked.

Lucas lifted his head. "It is, and the curtain moved. I think someone is looking out. We need to make this good." He cupped her chin and tipped her face upward, his thumb brushing against her cheek. "Is she one of the people parading men through your shop?"

Felina found it difficult to breathe, much less think, when Lucas's mouth was so close to hers. "Yes."

"Then let's make this good." He lowered his head and pressed his lips to hers, softly at first.

Felina's hands moved up his chest to lace behind his head as she pressed closer, her breasts smashing into his muscle-hardened chest.

His hands slipped over her lower back, not stopping until they cupped her ass, pulling her hips closer to his.

Her blood raced through her veins like molten lava, hot, thick and on fire, burning through her with such heat she could spontaneously combust at any moment.

Then he was setting her away from him. "That should about do it," he said with a grin.

Felina swayed. She put it down to a lack of oxygen after kissing for so very long. She drew in a breath and let it out. "Yup," she said, trying to make light of a kiss that had rocked her world. "That should keep Mrs. L. from pushing her grandson in my direction."

Lucas held out his hand. "Keys."

She frowned. "What? Why?" Her heart thumped against her chest. Was he going to take the kiss to the next step, follow her into her apartment and make mad, passionate love to her? Her heart swelled, and her core heated.

"I want to make sure your building is safe for you to enter."

"Oh." Like a balloon with a small hole pricked through the thin rubber, her heart deflated, and her core cooled. She dug in her purse for the keys and handed them to Lucas. "It's not necessary. I keep it locked securely when I leave."

"Consider it one of the perks of the job you hired me for. It's what I do. I make sure the building is safe for my client to enter." He took the key. "You live in your shop?"

She looked up. "In the apartment over the storefront. There are two entrances. One is around the side, and the other is in the back corner of the shop. We can go through the first floor."

Lucas inserted the key into the door lock and turned the key and handle. He pushed the door open and stepped inside.

Felina reached around him, flipped the switch on the wall, and the room filled with light.

The front room of the shop was filled with silk flower arrangements and a large refrigerator with a glass front. Inside the refrigerator were the arrangements made from real flowers. Most orders she'd worked on before closing that afternoon.

They'd be delivered the following day along with other orders she'd arrange in the morning.

"I like how homey this feels," Lucas said. "Reminds me of my mother's house. She loves flowers and always has fresh flowers in a vase on her table."

"My mother loves flowers as well," Felina followed Lucas through the door.

He waited for her, then turned to lock it behind them.

Felina's heart skipped a beat and then settled. He wasn't going to seduce her. He was only keeping her safe.

His loss.

She wondered how she could be so sexually aware of this man after breaking up with her boyfriend only a couple of short weeks ago.

Probably because they hadn't had sex in months. Sadly, she hadn't missed sex with Marty. How had she let their relationship wallow for so long without doing anything about it? She'd thought that perhaps she wasn't a sexually motivated woman or maybe even a little frigid.

Following Lucas into the flower shop, she was feeling anything but frigid.

The man had broad shoulders that pulled his T-shirt taut across his chest and emphasized the thickness of his biceps. As broad as his chest was, it narrowed significantly to a trim waist and tight ass.

Her mouth watered much like Pavlov's dog.

Lucas chose that moment to turn and caught her staring at his ass.

His lips curved. "Like what you see?"

Her cheeks flamed. "Don't know what you're talking about." She flipped her hair over her shoulder and started to pass him.

He held out an arm and clothes-lined her.

Her chest bumped into his arm. "What?"

Lucas shook his head. "Let me clear the building before you go any further."

"Seriously, it's okay. I've worked and lived in this building alone for the past five years. I've never encountered a boogeyman in all five of those years."

He pressed a finger to her lips. "Humor me."

She wanted to take the finger into her mouth. Instead, she backed away. "Fine. Do your thing. But make it quick. I have to be up at five in the morning to get my orders ready."

"Yes, ma'am," he said with a mock salute. Then he disappeared into the back of the shop. A moment later, footsteps sounded on the stairs leading up to her apartment.

Felina frowned, trying to remember if she'd made her bed and if she'd loaded the dirty dishes into the dishwasher that morning. Then she remembered the lace panties she'd hung to dry on the shower curtain rod and winced.

Then again, maybe those panties would inspire Lucas to stay a little longer.

No, no, no. Don't go there. Even if he wants it, we shouldn't.

She had to remind herself again that he was her employee, not a real date. She couldn't take advantage of him past the original agreement. Sex was not on the table.

Although, her worktable in the back of the shop was certainly big enough to accommodate them...

Felina closed her eyes. Hell, she'd gone way too long without satisfying an itch. It was time to break out B.O.B.—her battery-operated boyfriend.

Hmm. She'd need to change the batteries. They were so old they probably wouldn't work.

"Felina?"

Her eyes popped open.

Lucas stood in front of her, a smile playing at the corners of his lips. "Were you asleep on your feet or concentrating hard on something?"

Heat rose up her neck and suffused her cheeks. "Just thinking about what I had to accomplish before tomorrow's deliveries." Including finding batteries.

"Your shop and apartment are clear. I'll leave you to get some rest."

Like that was going to happen now with her hormones hopping and her libido screaming for release.

He walked toward the door. "Lock up after me."

She followed. "I will."

He held out her keys and dropped them into her open palm, curling his fingers around hers. "I'll be by early tomorrow."

She frowned. "Why?"

"A good boyfriend spends time with his girl. Now, give me your cell phone."

She dropped her keys into her purse, dug out her cell phone, and handed it to him. "Why do you need my cell phone?"

"A good boyfriend makes sure his girlfriend has his phone number saved to her favorites." He brought up her contact list, added his name and number and saved it to the top of her favorites above Marty's name.

"You want me to delete Marty?" he asked. "Or are you hoping he'll change his mind?"

"Delete him," she said. "Even if he did change his mind, I'm over him. I wouldn't take him back. I should've realized we weren't a good fit long before he felt the need to sneak around behind my back."

"Good. All the more reason for you to appear at his wedding with your boyfriend." He placed a call to the number he'd just entered. The phone in his pocket buzzed. He ended the call from her phone. "Now, I have your number as well." He handed her cell phone back to her.

She slipped it into her purse. "Thanks."

Lucas leaned forward, cupped the back of her

neck and lowered his head until his lips hovered over hers. "Mrs. Lebowitz is watching. Let's make it good." Then he kissed her so thoroughly, her fingers curled into his shirt and her toes curled in her shoes.

"Goodnight, Felina. Sleep tight," he whispered against her lips. Lucas unlocked the front door, stepped through it, and pulled it closed behind him. He waited until she twisted the deadbolt. Then he climbed into his big-ass truck and drove away.

Felina switched off the lights and stared out the window until Lucas's taillights disappeared.

Holy shit. What had she gotten herself into?

She'd only just been dumped by her long-term boyfriend. Now, here she was, lusting after her fake boyfriend.

A dark sedan drove slowly past her shop, turned on the next street and disappeared.

Felina turned and walked through the shop, the night lights she'd had installed giving her enough of a glow to make her way through without tripping over buckets of flowers or bumping into counters and tables. She climbed the stairs to her apartment, entered, then closed and locked her door.

She leaned her forehead against the cool wooden panel, trying not to think about the fact Lucas had been here minutes before. She could smell a hint of his cologne lingering in the air. Or was it lingering on her skin?

Felina squared her shoulders and went on a

search through her little apartment for B.O.B. She found the device in the bottom drawer of her nightstand, beneath old greeting cards from Marty, commemorating her birthday, Valentine's Day and other holidays. She dumped the cards into the trash and opened B.O.B.'s battery compartment.

Empty. Damn.

After a frantic search for fresh batteries with no luck, Felina took a cold shower and climbed into bed.

For the next hour, she tossed, turned, hugged her pillow, tossed it aside and lay awake, counting minutes. Hiring Lucas was supposed to relieve her anxieties and free her up to work without interruptions. Instead, it had ignited an entirely different set of emotions sure to keep her awake into the night.

About the time she was ready to give up, she nodded off.

No sooner had she closed her eyes when a sound jerked her back awake. She lay with her eyes open, listening. Had it been something in a dream?

Then it came again. A scraping sound of metal on metal—and was that a jiggle of a doorknob?

Felina sat up straight in bed.

The sound had come from the door leading to the staircase on the side of the building.

Felina rolled out of the bed, landing on her hands and knees on the opposite side of the bed from the exterior door.

The doorknob jiggled again.

She reached for her cell phone, pulling it from the charger on her nightstand. When she opened the screen, it came up with Lucas's contact page.

Without pausing to think, she called his number.

He answered on the first ring. "Missing me already?"

"Tell me you're outside my apartment door, testing my lock," she whispered. "Because if it's not you, someone is trying to get into my apartment."

CHAPTER 4

"Fuck," Lucas muttered. "I'm on my way. Stay on the phone." He'd just come out of a cold shower and dried off when his phone had buzzed. When he'd seen Felina's name flash across the screen, he'd smiled. If he wasn't mistaken, she'd been as affected by their kissing as he'd been.

He'd answered quickly before she could change her mind about calling him.

Her frightened voice had thrown the equivalent of a bucket of ice onto his libido.

Lucas put the cell phone on speaker while he dragged on jeans and his boots. He grabbed a T-shirt and his gun and ran out the door of his room in the Bayou Brotherhood Boarding House, where most of his teammates resided. It had been their home since they'd arrived and until they could secure alternate accommodations.

"I'm scared," Felina said.

"Where are your keys?" Lucas asked as he jumped up into his truck, tossing his T-shirt and gun onto the seat beside him.

"In my purse, hanging on a chair in the kitchenette."

"Does your car have an emergency button on the key fob?"

"I don't know," she answered.

"Can you get to your keys?" He spun out of the boarding house parking lot and gunned the accelerator.

"I think so," she said.

He could hear shuffling.

"Got them, and yes, there's a red button with a horn on it."

"Hit that button. Your horn will blare and draw attention to anyone around. That should scare the intruder away."

"The horn's blaring," she reported.

"Is he still working the doorknob?"

A loud crash sounded, and Felina's muffled squeal made Lucas's blood run cold. "What happened?" Lucas took a corner without slowing. The bed of his truck skidded sideways, fishtailing until he regained control.

"Shit, shit, shit," Felina's voice shook. "He broke the door jam and is kicking away the panels."

"I'm two minutes away. Can you get out the other door?"

"Heading that way now." A clunking sound was followed by a muttered curse and a door slamming.

"Felina!"

Muffled crashes sounded on the line.

"Felina!" He had almost reached Main Street when bright red and white lights flashed behind him, and a siren blared.

Good, Lucas thought; the parish police would follow him until he stopped in front of Felina's flower shop. They'd be his backup to neutralize Felina's intruder.

Mashing the accelerator all the way to the floor, Lucas raced down Main Street and skidded to a stop in front of Felina's building. Slamming the gear shift into park, he flew out of the driver's seat and ran up the stairs on the side of the building.

At the top, he eased around the doorframe, gun drawn, safety off. He stepped over the broken pieces of the door frame, reached inside and flipped on the light switch. When no one shot at him, he ducked low and slipped through the door into Felina's apartment.

Nothing moved. No one lunged for him or pointed a gun at Lucas as he made his way to the bathroom door. Drawers had been pulled out of the small dresser, clothes still on their hangers had been yanked from her closet and lay strewn across the floor. He nudged the bathroom door wider. The room was empty.

Lucas's pulse pounded. He didn't dare yell in case the intruder was still in the building. The door to the shop was closed.

As he reached for the knob, it turned.

He grabbed the knob and yanked it toward him. A glass vase appeared from around the doorframe and flew through the air.

Lucas ducked just in time. The vase crashed to the floor behind him.

Another vase sailed through the air.

"Felina!" he called out.

"Lucas?" Felina's head peered around the doorframe. "Oh, sweet Jesus." In a flurry of movement, she flung herself at him, another vase clutched in her hand. "I thought you were him."

"Yeah, it's me. I've got you. He's gone," he soothed, careful to point the gun in his hand away from her while he removed the vase from her fingers and laid it on the little kitchen table. Then, he held her close with his free hand.

"He was making so much noise in the apartment. I thought it was only a matter of time before he entered the shop. I had to do something, so I grabbed some vases. It was all I had." Her face pressed against his naked chest, and her arms wrapped around his waist, clutching him like a life preserver in a stormy sea.

"You did good," he said.

Footsteps pounded up the outside staircase.

A man in a sheriff's deputy uniform appeared in the doorway, his gun held out in front of him. "Put your hands up and step away from the woman."

"It's okay," Lucas said, following the deputy's commands, raising his hands above his head.

"Drop the gun!" the deputy yelled. "Drop the gun, or I'll shoot."

"I'll lay it on the floor." Lucas eased to the floor and laid down his weapon. Then he raised his empty hands.

"Step away from the woman," the deputy said.

"I have no intention of hurting her," Lucas said.

The deputy snorted. "Yeah, well, let the lady speak for herself."

Felina stepped around Lucas. "It's okay, Deputy Sarley. Lucas is my boyfriend. He came because I had an intruder. Did you see anyone running away from my building or a car driving away?"

"No, ma'am," Deputy Sarley said. "Just this guy speeding through town and stopping outside your place. You sure he isn't threatening you?"

Felina smiled and slipped her arm around Lucas's waist. "I'm positive. But you'll want to dust for prints. Whoever broke into my apartment trashed the place and, in the process, touched a lot of stuff. He might have left his prints on something."

"Is it all right for me to lower my arms?" Lucas

asked, refusing to lower his arms without permission in case the deputy got trigger-happy.

"Yes, sir." Deputy Sarley holstered his handgun.

As Lucas lowered his arms, Felina stepped away, crossing her arms over her breasts.

Lucas missed her arm around his waist and her body, dressed in that thin little nightgown, pressed against his. Damn, she had some fine legs.

Using his handheld radio, the deputy reported the break-in and the address. "They'll get our latent prints expert on it as soon as possible. It might be the morning before she can get here. I'll do some random drive-bys to keep an eye on the place until my shift ends and have whoever comes on duty next do the same. Do you have somewhere you can stay in the meantime?"

Felina nodded. "Can I gather some of my clothes?"

The deputy frowned. "I suppose. Just don't touch any hard surfaces. You wouldn't want to disturb any prints. And if you notice anything missing, make a list. I'll add it to my report."

"Right." Felina stepped toward the dresser drawers scattered across the floor.

Lucas wrapped an arm around her, stopping her before she'd gone too far. "You can't go any further barefooted. There's broken glass from the vases you threw all over the floor."

Felina nodded.

"Tell me what you want, and I'll get it for you," he offered.

"The jeans I left on the bathroom floor, the blue dress with the daisies, a couple of T-shirts if you can shake the glass off them and a handful of panties. Oh, and I'll need my pillow and a blanket."

He grabbed the blanket first and handed it to her.

She wrapped it around herself, covering the nearly see-through nightgown, which made Lucas happy. He didn't like the way Deputy Sarley kept staring at Felina, although he understood why. Lucas couldn't stop staring at her, either. Only he was her boyfriend, not the deputy, albeit her *fake* boyfriend.

With the pillow in hand, he stuffed the items she requested into the pillowcase and grabbed a pair of tennis shoes and a pair of sandals.

"I'll need my toiletries from the bathroom," she added. "I have a travel organizer hanging on the back of the door. It has everything I need in it except my toothbrush."

Lucas retrieved the organizer and the toothbrush and emerged from the bathroom. "Anything else?"

Felina sighed. "I'm sure I'll think of something else. But that should be enough to get me by for a day or two. At least until I can get back in here to clean up." She took the tennis shoes he handed her and slipped her feet into them. With a sad glance, she nodded. "I'm done here. We can leave through the shop door. I'll lock it behind us." She gave Deputy

Sarley a weak smile. "Thank you, deputy. Let me know if I need to file a statement."

The deputy nodded. "Yes, ma'am."

Lucas grabbed his gun from the floor where he'd laid it and followed Felina through the interior door. He waited on the landing while she locked the door and picked up her purse from the landing.

Lucas carried the stuffed pillowcase down the stairs.

Felina followed with the blanket wrapped around her.

They walked through the back work area and out to the reception area.

Lucas stopped at the front door and reached for the lock. "Is there someone you need to call before you show up on their doorstep?"

Felina shook her head. "No."

He twisted the lock and held the door for her, his gaze sweeping the surrounding buildings and street. "It might be nice to warn them before you barge in unannounced. People get shot that way."

When she didn't step through the door, he turned to see her standing firmly inside the shop.

Felina reached for the loaded pillowcase and held it close. "I'm not going anywhere."

Lucas frowned. "What do you mean? You can't stay in your apartment, it's not safe. You don't even have a door."

LUCAS

"I know." She swept her gaze around the shop. "I'll sleep on the floor in the shop."

Lucas blinked. "The hell you will."

She smiled. "I'll be all right. You heard Deputy Sarley. Between him and the next guy on duty, they'll make sure someone keeps an eye on the place until the latent print expert has a chance to dust my rooms upstairs. Then I'll have my carpenter replace the door with a metal one. I'll be fine."

"Can't you stay with your mother or a friend?"

Felina shook her head. "I have to be at work at five o'clock in the morning. My mother doesn't get up before ten—and I don't want her to know about the break-in. She'll insist I move back in with her."

"Is that such a bad idea?" he asked.

"The worst. I love her, but I can't live with her. She drives me batshit crazy."

He ran a hand through his hair. "You have friends."

She shook her head. "I'm staying here."

"You can't be serious."

"I assure you, I'm very serious," she said.

"You can stay with me at the boarding house," he suggested. "You can have the bed. I'll sleep on the floor."

Her head continued to shake. "I'm staying here. I didn't spend the last five years building my business to have someone scare me away from it. What if he comes back and destroys my work? This is my livelihood. I'm not the only one depending on the income generated here. I support my mother as well. Without my shop, I have nothing. I don't have a college education. I'd be forced to get a low-paying job in the city and rent an apartment I couldn't afford as well as pay for my mother's mortgage and utilities. I sank everything into this place. I'm not leaving."

Lucas took her hands in his. "Sweetheart, this is your life. *Things* can be replaced. *Buildings* can be rebuilt. *You* can't be replaced or rebuilt if you're destroyed."

Felina's jaw hardened.

Lucas wasn't liking this.

"I'm staying." She lifted her chin. "And tomorrow, I'll buy a gun."

He was fighting a losing battle with this one. "Have you ever fired a gun?"

Her brow furrowed. "No, but I can learn."

"The last thing you need to do is purchase a weapon that could get you killed."

"I'm smart. I learn quickly."

"I'm sure you are and can, and I'd be happy to teach you. But it takes time." He sighed. "Are you sure you don't want to stay with a friend or relative?"

She shook her head, her mouth set in a firm line. "I need to be here. I have a lot of work to do and orders to place for several big events coming up, including Trish's wedding."

"Okay." He knew what he had to do. "Wait here."

Lucas left through the front door, strode out to his truck and opened the rear door. He grabbed the go-bag and sleeping bag he kept tucked behind the seat and returned to the shop.

Felina's brow dipped low as she inspected the items he carried. "I don't need your sleeping bag. I have a blanket and pillow, it's all I need."

He dropped the go-bag and sleeping bag on the floor, turned and locked the door. "You might not need it, but I do." Lucas faced her.

Her frown deepened.

He touched a finger to the area between her eyes. "You're going to get frown lines if you keep that up." He slung his go-bag over his shoulder, tucked the sleeping bag beneath his arm and looked around. "Are we camping out in the workroom or up front?"

"*I'm* camping out in the workroom." She poked her finger at his chest. "*You're* going back to wherever you're staying."

He caught her finger and brought it up to press his lips to the tip. "As your boyfriend, it wouldn't be right of me to leave you alone after someone broke into your apartment. If you want people to buy into our relationship, I have to stay. And, I have a gun and know how to use it. I'd say that's a win-win all around. Less the fact we'll be sleeping on a hard floor. But then, I've slept in worse places." He marched to the back of the shop and started rearranging the worktables to make more room for them to stretch out on the floor.

She followed slowly. "You don't have to do this."

"Yes, I do." He untied the strap around his sleeping bag and unrolled and unzipped it. Then he spread it across the floor, wide enough for two people to sleep side by side. He laid his go-bag out like a pillow and stretched out on one side of the bag. "It's getting late. Do you mind turning off the light?"

She stood for a moment longer, frowning.

"Or leave it on. You might not want to be in the dark after having someone break into your apartment. It's up to you. I can sleep with it on or off." He rolled onto his side away from her. "Good night, Felina."

He closed his eyes, his ears on high alert for her movements.

"This is not how I planned to spend the night," she muttered.

"Me either," he agreed.

The shuffle of sneakers sounded nearby. A moment later, the light clicked off, throwing the workroom into semi-darkness, broken only by the glow of the red exit sign over the rear door and a couple of strategically placed nightlights on either side of the room. After the rustle of the blanket and items of clothing being dumped out of the pillowcase they shared with her pillow, Felina settled on the floor beside Lucas.

She lay stiffly beside him without any part of her body touching his.

Then she moved and spread part of the blanket over him.

"You don't have to share," he said. "My body runs hot."

"The air conditioner gets cold in here at night," she said.

Rather than refuse her kind gesture, he said, "Thanks."

"Thank you for coming to my rescue," she whispered.

His lips pressed together. "I wish I could've been here sooner."

"It all worked out." She chuckled. "And to think, I wouldn't have had your number to call if you hadn't stepped out the back door of the bar."

Lucas rolled onto his back and stared up at the ceiling. "And I wouldn't have gone looking for you if I hadn't been determined to buy you a drink."

"You never did get to try your pickup lines on me," she said.

He grinned. "No, I didn't."

She turned toward him. "Since I'm a captive audience, you can try now. Shoot."

"Okay, here's one." He grinned. "Do you believe in love at first sight? Or should I walk by you again?" When she didn't comment, he asked, "Did you like that one?"

"On a scale of one to ten..." she said, "I'd call that lame."

"How about this one..." He paused for effect. "Do you have a map? Because I get lost in your eyes."

"Better," she commented. "Kind of sweet without being sleazy."

"Since you're a florist and all into flowers, I had some I thought you'd appreciate."

She yawned. "I'm listening."

"Are you a garden?" he said. "Because I'm digging you."

"Cute."

"Along those same lines..." he started. "Are you a garden? Because I want to get lost in you."

"Borderline sleazy."

"If you were a flower, I'd pick you."

"Meh. Flowers die when you pick them," she said. "Try again."

He turned on his side to face her. "What would I say if I wanted a flower like you to kiss me?"

She looked toward him, her brow creasing. "I don't know, what would you say?"

He flopped onto his back and grinned. "Plant one on me."

For a moment, she didn't say anything. Then she giggled a little.

The sound warmed him. "Liked that one, did you?"

"No." She giggled again. A little longer this time.

"I'm just picturing some poor woman sitting beside you at a bar, rolling her eyes." Her giggles continued. "Honey," she said, choking on laughter, "you might be single for a lot longer with lines like that." She pressed a hand to her belly, laughing so hard that tears streamed down her cheeks.

Her laughter was contagious and had Lucas chuckling at first, then laughing along with her.

When Felina's giggles subsided, the tears continued to flow, body shaking with silent sobs.

"Whoa, babe, what's this?" Lucas reached for her and pulled her into his arms. "I didn't mean to make you cry."

"You didn't." She scrubbed at the tears that wouldn't stop. "I don't know what's wrong with me. I never cry."

His arms tightened around her, and he pressed his lips to her forehead. "You've had a rough night. Hell, you've had a rough couple of weeks. You're allowed a few tears."

"Tears are for weaklings," Felina sniffed noisily. "I'm not a weakling."

"Tears are like a safety valve. It's your body and soul's way of releasing overwhelming pressure. You're like a pressure cooker. When the pressure builds up, it's released in steam. In your case, it's released in tears."

Felina sniffed again and rubbed at her damp cheeks.

Lucas kissed the tip of her nose. "It helps release stress, ease grief and even help you process extreme joy."

"Huh?" She looked up at him. "Why would you need help processing joy?"

"Think about the mothers giving birth. They work so hard physically to bring another life into the world. When they finally meet their babies, many of them cry tears of joy."

"And relief."

"That too," he said with a grin. "The point is...tears are a release. Sometimes, you have to let them go to relieve the pressure inside."

"Mmmm. I think you're right. And laughter helps, too." She rested her cheek against his naked chest. "Thank you."

"For what?"

"For terrible pickup lines." She yawned. "Apparently, I needed...the laughter...and...the tears." Her voice faded off, her breathing grew deeper, and Felina slept in Lucas's arms. He didn't care the floor was hard, or that his arm was getting numb. He didn't want to move a single muscle and disturb this woman's sleep.

For the past few weeks, he'd spent more money on flower arrangements than he had his entire life, trying to get this woman's attention so that he could ask her out. He hadn't known she'd had a boyfriend because he'd never seen her with another man.

Marty had to be a complete fool to dump her for another woman.

Lucas had seen how good Felina was with people, no matter if they were old, young, black, white, male or female, grief-stricken or celebrating. She brightened their days with her floral arrangements and her smile.

His teammates had teased him about his pursuit of this woman, telling him she wasn't interested and that he should move on. She'd never date him.

Maybe not. But she was his girlfriend for the next two weeks. That gave him exactly two weeks to convince her that he was worth seeing for a more extended period or that they really didn't belong together.

He was aiming for the first scenario, already convinced she was perfect for him.

More than his desire to be with Felina was his growing concern over her safety. His arm tightened around her as he mulled over what had happened and what could have happened.

First, she'd been shoved off the back landing at the Crawdad Hole. Then, someone had forcibly broken into her apartment and trashed the place. Had she been in the room at the time the intruder broke through the door, would he have hurt her?

Lucas was glad Felina had gotten out of the apartment before the man had broken through and even happier that the car alarm had helped to end his reign of destruction before he'd gotten to the door to the shop. The vases she'd thrown at Lucas wouldn't have done much to slow down the attacker.

What if the man had broken through the door while Felina had been dead asleep and too groggy to think fast? What if Felina hadn't called Lucas, and he hadn't reminded her of the emergency horn feature on her key fob?

The night could have had a much different conclusion.

Until they found the man who'd broken into her apartment, Lucas wouldn't leave Felina's side even if he had to sleep with her and not make love to her.

His attraction to Felina wasn't all about sex. He was content to lie there holding her, making no move to take their physical contact to the next level.

He wasn't averse to making love with Felina, but it had to be something she wanted, not something she felt obligated to give. He'd never force a woman or take advantage of her when she was in a difficult emotional state.

When they made love...and they would...it would be with wholehearted mutual consent.

And it would be beautiful, perfect and well worth the wait.

In the meantime, his body ached with a need he could not satisfy until then.

With his gun lying within reach, Lucas willed himself to relax and sleep. Granted, sleep would be light, with one eye open, his senses on alert. If the attacker returned, Lucas would be ready.

He could kick himself for driving away earlier, leaving Felina alone. He should have been there for her when her attacker busted down her door.

Instead, the man had escaped, leaving behind a huge mess of empty drawers, their contents flung across the floor.

Had he been looking for something? If so, what? Hopefully, he'd found it and left, never to return.

In the morning, they'd go over everything that had happened that evening. Though the shoving incident seemed separate from the break-in, Lucas had a feeling they were connected. How? He didn't know. But he sure as hell would find out.

In the meantime, he'd carry his gun and stick with Felina like a second skin.

It was his job.

More than that...

It was Felina.

He couldn't let anything happen to the woman he hoped would someday bear his children.

After Felina's recent breakup with jerkface Marty, Lucas had an uphill battle ahead of him to bring the woman of his dreams around to believing he was the man of her dreams.

As she lay nestled in his arms, hope blossomed. At least he could hold her while she was dreaming. Maybe those dreams would one day include him.

CHAPTER 5

SOMETHING BRUSHED across Felina's forehead, stirring her awake. She blinked her eyes open to semi-darkness and an unfamiliar ceiling. As she shifted her gaze around the room, the realization came into focus.

She lay on the floor of her florist shop workroom.

Felina turned her face, her cheek pressing into taut flesh stretched over hard muscles.

What the hell?

She sat up straight and looked down at the man leaning up on his elbow, his dark hair tousled, a grin spreading across his face.

"I hated to wake you, but you said you wanted to be up early so that you could work on your floral arrangements."

Felina nodded, her gaze sweeping the room, taking in the buckets of fresh flowers waiting for her to craft into tasteful bouquets for her customers. "I forgot to set an alarm." Her eyes narrowed. "Oh, wait. Because my alarm clock is upstairs on my nightstand in my ransacked apartment." She looked at Lucas as he sat up. "It wasn't a bad dream?"

He reached out and brushed a strand of her hair back behind her ear.

His fingers brushing against her skin sparked an electric current that spread heat throughout her body, pooling at her core.

Her breath hitched, and she almost leaned into his palm. Fortunately, she caught herself short, appalled at how easily being with him could get out of hand.

She flung aside the blanket and leaped to her feet. "I have to get to work, and I need this space for my worktables."

He rose, gathered his sleeping bag and rolled it into a tight bundle, securing the ties around it. After he tucked it into a corner, he helped Felina move the tables back where they belonged.

"Why don't you get dressed while I find some breakfast for the two of us," he said.

"I don't usually eat this early. But coffee would be wonderful. I keep the coffee corner fully stocked out front for me, my delivery driver and customers."

"I'll get the coffee going while you get dressed," he said. "When your driver arrives, I'll duck out for food."

"Thanks." Felina gathered the clothes she'd need

and hurried into the bathroom that doubled as a storeroom for cleaning supplies.

After splashing water on her face, Felina brushed her teeth and dried off with a paper towel. She pulled the baby doll nightgown over her head. The break-in the previous night had her rethinking sleeping in sexy, sheer garments. Perhaps, as a single woman, she'd be better off opting for oversized T-shirts that covered everything important. Her mother's words came back to haunt her. *Always wear fresh underwear. You never know when you could be in an accident or end up in a hospital.*

Thankfully, she'd had on fresh underwear, but she wouldn't have wanted her attacker to catch her in the skimpy nightgown.

She hung it on a hook on the wall and pulled on the jeans she'd worn the night before. There was something in the back pocket. She barely remembered Gisele slipping her hand back there before they'd left the Crawdad Hole.

Felina brought out a plastic packet and realized her friend had armed her with a condom.

Heat filled her chest and cheeks. Her friend had assumed she'd sleep with the handsome Delta Force soldier. She hadn't been completely wrong.

Yes, Felina had slept with Lucas. On a hard floor. Nothing had happened that would have necessitated the use of the condom. The man had been a perfect gentleman.

"Sadly," Felina murmured and tucked the packet back into her pocket. It was just as well that nothing sexy had occurred. She'd only just gotten out of a bad relationship. Even if Lucas wasn't on the payroll, he could only be her rebound. Right?

She dug through the stack of clothes she'd had Lucas gather, a frown forming.

No bra.

Damn.

Her girls weren't huge, but her nipples tended to be pointy under the air conditioning. However, Felina didn't have time to worry about the lack of a bra. She pulled a navy-blue T-shirt over her head and tucked it into the waistband of her jeans. Grabbing her socks, she exited the bathroom to find Lucas coming toward her with a mug full of steaming brew.

"Oh, thank God," she said and accepted the mug. "I can do without a lot of things, but coffee isn't one of them." She sipped the hot drink carefully, letting the rich liquid soothe her nerves. A couple of sips later, she was ready to face whatever the day had to throw at her.

She set the mug on the counter, dropped into a chair and pulled on her socks and tennis shoes. "The bathroom's all yours. It's not equipped with a shower on this level, but you can shave and use the toilet."

"Thanks," Lucas said. "I'll leave the door open in case you need me."

"You don't have to do that. I'll be fine for a few minutes. Besides, you're only a few feet away."

His brow dipped low. "The sun hasn't even come up. Anyone could sneak up on your shop in the dark."

"I'll be fine," she said. "Go."

Lucas reluctantly entered the bathroom and eased the door closed. The expression on his face was anything but happy about letting her out of his sight.

Felina smiled. The man took his job seriously, which made Felina glad to have him providing her security as well as pretending to be her boyfriend/lover. Until they found the man who'd trashed her apartment, Felina couldn't feel comfortable alone.

She checked the computer for the orders due for delivery that day and started to work.

While Lucas was still in the bathroom, a loud knock sounded on the door in the front reception area.

Felina shot a glance toward the closed bathroom door, debating whether or not to answer the knock. Another knock helped her make the decision to answer the door.

She hurried from the back work area to the front customer reception area. A figure in a uniform stood on the other side of the glass door.

Felina grinned when she saw that it was her friend, Shelby Taylor.

Felina unlocked the front door and let Shelby inside. "What brings you out so early in the morning?

"You." Shelby wrapped her arms around Felina, hugged her and then stepped back. "I didn't know your apartment had been broken into until I came on duty. I hurried over as soon as I heard. Tell me what happened."

Felina gave her friend a short version of what had occurred the night before.

"Why didn't you come stay with me?" Shelby asked.

"It was late. I didn't want to disturb anyone, so I stayed in the shop."

Shelby frowned. "Are you crazy? What if the intruder came back?"

"Deputy Sarley assured me a unit would come by often to check on me." Felina shrugged. "I wasn't too worried."

"But you were alone. It only takes a few minutes for someone to break through a door. You shouldn't have been alone."

As if on cue, Lucas emerged from the workroom, wearing a black T-shirt, his hair wet and face clean-shaven. "Good morning, Deputy Taylor."

Shelby's eyes widened. "Okay. I see why you stayed." Her lips twitched. "I guess hiring Lucas was a good idea after all, huh?"

Lucas shot a glance from Felina to Shelby. "Can I get you some coffee, deputy?"

"No, I have a cup in my unit. I just wanted to check on Felina. I'm glad you're with her. I've learned no matter how capable you are at defending yourself, it's nice when someone has your back—and she needs someone to have her back, especially after last night with the incident at the Crawdad Hole and the break-in. Speaking of the incident at the bar, it's another reason I came to check on you."

Felina frowned. "Why? Did you find the guy who shoved me or the mysterious SUV without a license plate?"

"We're not sure. A couple of Fontenot cousins were out frog giggin' in the bayou early this morning and came across a body."

Felina gasped and pressed a hand to her chest. "Anyone we know?"

Shelby shook her head. "No one I know."

Felina's eyes widened. "You think it might be the guy who shoved me?"

"I don't know. Did you get a good look at him before he got into the SUV?"

"Maybe," Felina said.

"I saw him," Lucas said. "I'm confident I can tell you if the body is the guy from the bar or not."

Felina nodded. "And he didn't get into that SUV of his own volition. A big guy shoved him in. I wouldn't doubt the man ended up in the bayou."

Shelby's lips thinned. "Which is why I came to you. The body the Fontenots found hadn't started decomposing yet, from what the coroner said. They took him to the parish coroner's office. When you get a chance, could you swing by and look him over? He might be the guy who shoved you. In which case, we'll need to find the people in that SUV."

Felina looked around the shop. "I have orders I need to get out before ten o'clock. Can it wait until then?"

Shelby nodded. "Absolutely. The coroner will be conducting the autopsy to determine the cause of death. I'll let them know you'll be stopping by to see if you can identify the man as the one from the Crawdad Hole last night. I've also asked for the surveillance videos from last night. I'm hoping I could see when your guy came and left and maybe get a look at the men from the SUV."

"I'd be interested in those videos as well," Felina said. "The guy who shoved me was rude and callous, but I almost felt sorry for him when the big guy shoved him into the back seat of that SUV. It didn't look like an invitation."

"Let me know when you're free," Shelby said. "I'll meet you at the coroner's office." She looked up at Lucas. "You'll be with her now, 24/7?"

Lucas nodded. "Yes, ma'am."

"Good. I don't know what's going on yet, but I'm concerned that our girl is being targeted. Deputy

81

Sarley said whoever broke into your apartment ransacked it like he was looking for something."

Felina nodded. "Had he been looking for me, he wouldn't have stopped to dump my dresser and kitchen drawers or clear my closet of everything I had hanging inside." She frowned. "But what do I have that he'd want? I'm just a florist. I don't have any expensive jewelry or state secrets. It doesn't make sense."

"Good question." Shelby turned to go. "I'll be looking for answers. Stay safe and let me know when you're headed for the coroner's office."

"Will do," Felina locked the door behind Shelby and watched as the deputy drove away. When she glanced at the clock, she gasped. "Shoot! My driver will be here soon, and I'm not ready." She ran for her workroom and worked in a flurry of motion, tackling one arrangement after another.

Lucas stood back, offering to help where he could. She had him handing her vases, stems and ribbon whenever he was closest. If she needed help holding something in place, he was there, taking directions without question. When the latent print specialist arrived, Lucas showed her up to the apartment and waited while she dusted for prints. When she was done, she left her card with Lucas and drove away. Felina hadn't said more than hello to the woman, instead focusing on all she had to accomplish.

By the time her delivery guy, Bruno Brun, arrived, she'd worked through ninety percent of the order he was to deliver that morning.

"Heard you had some trouble last night," Bruno commented. "Something about a break-in...?"

"Yup," Felina said. "Lucas can fill you in. Lucas, this is Bruno. Bruno, this is Lucas, my boyfriend."

Out of the corner of her eye, Felina saw Bruno's eyebrow rise up his dark forehead. He held out his hand to Lucas. "Dude, you'll have to fill me in on a lot more than the break-in."

"Let Felina do her thing," Lucas said, drawing the driver toward the front of the shop where they'd staged the deliveries. "I'll tell you what I know while we load the orders in the van."

While Lucas helped load the arrangements in the van, Felina finished the last three bouquets, wondering how Lucas painted their relationship status. She'd have to make sure she had the same story if they wanted everyone to believe they were really in a relationship.

After the break-in, Felina was beginning to believe her ego and the effort to deflect the match-making mamas with her little fake relationship were inconsequential compared to having her apartment ransacked and finding a body in the bayou.

She breathed a sigh as she carried the last vase to the van. At least she'd managed to fill the orders for delivery. She could work the others due to be picked up later that afternoon after she visited the coroner's office.

A shiver rippled across her skin as she stood in the morning sun, the southern Louisiana heat and humidity wrapping around her like a thick cloak.

Lucas slipped an arm around her waist and pulled her close. "Mrs. Lebowitz is looking."

"Seems so stupid."

"That she's looking?"

"That I'm even remotely worried about what the neighbors think." She turned to face him. "Someone broke into my apartment last night. Now, a man is dead. Why should I even give a damn about what Mrs. Lebowitz sees?"

Lucas smoothed a strand of her hair off her cheek. "You shouldn't give a damn." He bent and brushed a kiss across her forehead. "What's important is that you're safe." He kissed the tip of her nose.

Her breath caught and held in her throat. "Then why are you kissing me?" she whispered.

"Because I can't resist." He smiled softly, his lips hovering over hers. "You're the ultimate flower to my bee. I'm drawn to your nectar."

His lips claimed hers in a kiss that swept her away from the break-in, the shop, the impending wedding and Bayou Mambaloa. It was just her and Lucas.

When he lifted his head, she swayed, leaning into him.

God, she could get used to this.

He grinned. "No comment on my pickup line?"

She frowned, her brain still in a lust fog. "Pickup line?"

He cocked an eyebrow. "Flower...bee...nectar?"

As his words sank in, her lips quivered. The man was too cute for her heart. If she wasn't careful, she'd fall for him. She'd do her best to guard her heart and to keep him in check. "Oh. Yeah. About that..." She reached up and patted his cheek. "One hundred percent corny. Try again."

Despite her judgment, she'd found the line absolutely adorable. If they were in a real relationship, she'd have...what?

Kissed him like they were the only two people on the face of the earth, completely blocking out everyone and everything around them?

Oh, wait. That's what she'd done.

Felina backed out of his arms, forcing a smile. "Let's go to the coroner's office. I need to get back as soon as possible." She turned and walked back into the shop, still talking. "Trish will be in after lunch to discuss changes to her floral arrangements. I'm also doing the flowers for Colonial Day in Bayou Mambaloa. I need to visit some of the old plantation houses that will be open for the event. They all want massive flower arrangements for their entry halls and sitting rooms. Then there's the matter of cleaning my apartment so I don't have to sleep on the floor tonight." She stopped halfway to the workroom. "Shoot. I need to call a carpenter to replace my door."

"That's a lot," Lucas said. "If I can help in any way, let me."

"Be careful what you wish for," she said.

"If you have a phone number for the carpenter, I can make that call. He'll probably want you to pick a door."

"I don't care what kind of door it is as long as it can't be kicked in. And that means replacing the doorframe with something indestructible as well." She scrolled through her contacts on her cell phone, found Richard Smithson's number and shared it to Lucas's phone. "I know it's not your responsibility to organize my life, and it's not part of your job description," she laughed, "nor is pretending to be my boyfriend, but I appreciate all you're doing for me. I don't know what I would've done if you hadn't come looking for me at the Crawdad Hole."

"It was my pleasure," he said. "Even though I suspected you were intent on skipping out on me rather than letting me buy you a drink."

Her cheeks heated. "I was. And what a mistake that was. If I'd just let you buy me that drink, I wouldn't have been standing on the back landing when that guy came running out."

His eyebrows waggled. "But then, you might not have seen how useful I could be and wouldn't have hired me to be your fake boyfriend."

"And I wouldn't have had your phone number to call during the break-in." She shook her head. "Maybe things happened the way they did for a reason."

He cupped her cheek in his palm. "Maybe."

She gazed up at him, quickly getting lost in his eyes. "Shall we?" she whispered.

"Mmm-huh," he said, leaning closer.

She wanted to kiss him so badly it scared her. Felina placed a finger across his lips and stepped back. "Go to the coroner's office?"

"Oh, yeah." He straightened, his lips quirking at the corners. "I'll drive."

She didn't argue. It was bad enough that she had to go there and look at a dead man. "Give me ten minutes to check the order system and straighten my workspace."

He nodded. "I'll call the carpenter and get that ball rolling."

She went to her computer in the corner of the work area and brought up her order system.

Lucas called the number she'd shared. While waiting for an answer, he checked the lock on the back door of the shop, then strode into the front reception area. "I'd like to speak with Richard Smithson." The rest of his conversation faded into the other room.

While Felina had been busy loading the delivery van, three more orders had come in for afternoon pickups. She checked her phone messages. Three telemarketers and one unknown caller. She listened to the unknown caller's message.

"This is Brenda Crabtree from the Cypress Hill Plantation. I'm preparing for the annual Colonial Day in Bayou Mambaloa and would like to order special arrangements for the event. Could we arrange a time for you to visit my home so that we can discuss what I have in mind? My apologies for the short notice. The sooner you can come, the better."

Felina jotted down her phone number, excited that she was being considered for each of the plantation houses in the parish. She'd been to some of the historical homes as a child on Colonial Day. Until now, she hadn't been entrusted with providing the floral arrangements for the event. Her heart swelled with pride that her reputation had grown over the past five years to the point she was being commissioned to provide the flowers for the big event.

Lucas entered the workroom. "The carpenter will stop by after lunch to measure and see what he'll need to complete the job. He has a metal exterior door kit with a metal frame he'd ordered for another job. The customer changed his mind and opted for something different. He'd planned on returning the door for a refund, but if it works, he thinks he can complete the installation today. He might have to come back to finish the trim and paint another day, but you could have a door with a lock by the end of the day."

"Seriously?" Felina logged off her computer and grabbed her purse. "I could be sleeping in my own bed tonight?"

"He couldn't make any promises, but knock on wood, it could happen." Lucas walked with her to the front entrance and held the door.

She flipped the sign in the window from OPEN to CLOSED, stepped outside, pulled the door closed and locked it.

Lucas held out his arm. "Ready?"

She heaved a sigh and looped her hand through the crook in his elbow. "As ready as I'll ever be to see a dead body."

He helped her up into the truck and closed the door.

She pulled out her cell phone and texted Shelby that they were on their way to the coroner's office.

They passed through town in silence. The coroner's office was on the west side of town, tucked between the animal shelter and the parish maintenance site.

A sheriff's vehicle stood in the parking lot.

Lucas parked beside it, dropped down from the driver's seat and hurried around in time to help Felina to the ground.

She drew a deep breath, squared her shoulders and walked toward the building.

Lucas captured her hand in his, squeezed it reassuringly then let go.

He opened the door and held it for her to pass through.

Shelby waited inside. "Hey," she said. "You feeling all right?"

Felina shrugged. "Sure."

Shelby gave her a twisted smile. "First dead body?"

Felina nodded. "First, since my father's funeral."

"I remember," Shelby said. "That was awful."

Felina's mother had wailed and tried to crawl into the casket with her husband, shocking the entire community.

"I got a pretty good look at him at the Crawdad Hole," Lucas said. "I can do this. You don't have to."

Felina shook her head. "Two witnesses are better than one."

Lucas rested a hand on the small of her back and walked down the hallway, following Shelby.

She stopped at a door, knocked lightly, then pushed the door open. "Dr. Rhodes, it's Deputy Taylor. I have two people here to identify the body."

"Send them in," a voice called out.

Shelby tipped her head toward Lucas and Felina.

They followed her into the examination room.

A man in a white coat stood beside a stainless-steel table with a body stretched across its surface, half-draped in a white sheet.

Felina's stomach roiled at the overwhelming scents, one of which resembled stagnant bayou water. She pinched her nose closed and crossed to the table.

The man on the table was chalky white and naked beneath the sheet.

She'd only seen her guy's face for a few brief seconds when the big guy had spun him around and shoved him into the SUV. Looking at the guy on the table, she wasn't sure.

"It's him," Lucas said. "See the scar on the right side of his mouth?"

Felina looked closer. "I see it."

"I remember it because it makes him look like he's sneering."

The scar wasn't large, but it was enough to make him appear to be sneering.

"He has the right color hair," Felina said. "I remember it being lighter than the guy who threw him into the SUV. And curly."

"Thank you, Dr. Rhodes," Shelby said.

He acknowledged with a brief nod and went back to his examination of the victim.

"Do you know who he is?" Felina turned with Shelby as they headed for the exit.

"Not yet." Shelby left the exam room, waited for Felina and Lucas to pass through the doorway and then pulled the door closed. "He was found naked in the bayou. No form of identification on or near him.

We're running his prints and face through available databases." Shelby led the way down the hallway and out of the building. She stopped beside her work vehicle. "If he was murdered—which we suspect he was—Felina could identify the man who forced him into the SUV. He might not want to leave that thread hanging."

Felina shivered. "Then why did he stop short of finding me in my apartment? He had enough time to kill me, but he spent it going through my things."

Shelby shrugged. "I don't know. Maybe he thought you were with our dead guy. That he might have left something in your apartment they want. I hope that his identity will give us a clue."

"You'll let us know when you figure out who he is?" Lucas asked.

Shelby nodded as she pulled open the driver's door. "I will. I'm meeting with Rene DeRoche after I leave here to review the video surveillance footage from the Crawdad Hole."

"We're going there when we leave here," Lucas said.

"Then I'll see you there," Shelby slid into her vehicle and backed out of the parking lot.

As Lucas held the door for Felina, she said, "I need to get back to work."

"We'll stop long enough to pick up some food to take back to your shop," Lucas said. "We skipped breakfast; we're not skipping lunch."

Felina glared at Lucas. "Bossy much?" When her belly rumbled, her glare lost some of its oomph.

Lucas cocked an eyebrow.

"Okay." She pressed a hand to her empty stomach. "We'll stop for carryout and a look at that surveillance video."

Lucas let out an overly exaggerated breath. "Thank you." He climbed into the truck and followed Shelby's sheriff's vehicle to the Crawdad Hole, which was just opening up for lunch.

Though she didn't like being told what to do, Felina appreciated that Lucas was looking out for her. She hadn't had someone to really look out for her since she was eleven when her father had died in an oil rig accident, and her mother had fallen apart.

Not that she was relinquishing control of her life to the man, but it felt good to have someone care whether or not she'd had a meal that day.

So, she only had Lucas for two weeks. Why not enjoy the attention? It didn't matter whether it was real or fake. He'd be gone after the job ended.

The wedding would be over, her life would return to normal, and she'd go on as if Lucas had never been a part of it.

Yeah, only it wasn't that simple. Not when she was making the colossal mistake of falling for the hired hand.

CHAPTER 6

Lucas left Felina with Shelby in Rene DeRoche's office, going over the footage from the night before.

He sat at the bar, talking with the bartender and owner of the Crawdad Hole while he waited for the order he'd placed for a hamburger and French fries for him and sliced brisket sandwich for Felina.

"As soon as Deputy Taylor asked about the video surveillance footage from last night," Rene, the bartender, said, "I went over it myself, looking for anything that might help us identify the man who pushed Felina or the people who forced him into that SUV."

"What did you see?" Lucas asked.

"I saw about what you saw last night," Rene said as he wiped down the bar. "The man who went out the back door did appear, coming in the front door a little earlier, but I couldn't see what he arrived in.

It appeared as if he'd entered the parking lot on foot."

"What about the SUV?" Lucas asked.

"Other than it being big and black with tinted windows, it had no other identifying marks. I didn't recognize the big man who got out to manhandle the other guy. The camera did get a clear view of his face." Rene shrugged. "Maybe the sheriff's department can run his image through some facial recognition database."

"Sounds like these guys aren't from around here."

Rene shook his head. "We get a lot of folks visiting from New Orleans. Mostly, people wanting to fish or get a taste of the bayou by taking an airboat ride, seeing alligators or enjoying the festivals we have. In fact, Colonial Day is coming up in a week and a half. There will be a surge of visitors in Bayou Mambaloa for that."

"Felina mentioned several big events coming up."

Rene nodded. "Colonial Day is one of them. Tourism is one of the biggest industries in our parish. Businesses are gearing up, increasing inventory and sinking money into preparations. News of a murder could keep people from coming. It could be devastating to the local economy if an event is canceled."

"If a murderer is still out there, everyone is at risk until he's captured and removed from the area," Lucas said.

"Absolutely," Rene said. "The sooner they do that,

the sooner everything can get back to normal. I just hate to think one of my customers was picked up on my property, murdered and dumped in the bayou. That back door isn't locked from the inside because it's considered an emergency exit. People can't come in through that door, but I can't stop them going out."

A member of Rene's kitchen staff emerged from the kitchen carrying a bag emitting wonderful scents.

Lucas's belly rumbled loudly. He laughed as he gathered the bag.

Rene grinned. "I had them throw in extra French fries."

"Thanks." Lucas stood. "Hopefully, we'll sort this out before the events take place."

Felina emerged from the hallway leading to the back of the bar and Rene's office. "Ready?"

Lucas held up the bag of dinners. "Ready."

"I want to stop by one of the Colonial homes on the way back to the shop." She grimaced. "Well, not exactly on the way. Still, I need to meet with this customer so that I can document the dimensions and contents of the arrangements she needs. I want to include her requests in the order I'll make today."

"We can do that," Lucas said as they reached his truck.

Felina climbed in and pulled out her cell phone. "I'm texting the homeowner now."

Lucas rounded the truck and slid into the driver's seat.

Felina glanced up from her cell phone with a smile. "Mrs. Crabtree said it's okay to come now."

Minutes later, Lucas pulled up to a closed gate with a keypad. He pressed the talk button and waited.

"Felina Faivre to see Mrs. Crabtree," Lucas announced.

No one responded, but the gate slid open, allowing Lucas to drive his big truck through.

Lucas studied the perfectly manicured landscaping and natural elements. The trees parted ahead, revealing a two-story colonial mansion with wraparound porches on both levels. Ancient oak trees lined the driveway up to the house.

"It hasn't changed much since the last time I was here as a kid." Felina sat forward, her eyes shining. "Perhaps it has a new coat of paint on the outside. I can't wait to see the inside again."

Lucas stopped in front of the house and shifted into park. He climbed down and hurried around to help Felina out.

She was so intently studying the house that she missed her footing on the running board and tumbled into Lucas's arms.

He caught her and held her close until she had her feet firmly beneath her. Then he pressed a brief kiss to her lips and turned toward the mansion in time to see a woman step out onto the porch.

Mrs. Crabtree wore a cream-colored skirt suit and matching shoes. Her hair was swept up in a neat twist, and her face was expertly made up. She looked like she'd be more at home in New York City than in Bayou Mambaloa.

"I should've dressed a little more professionally," Felina murmured under her breath, wrapping her arms over her chest as though she were cold.

Lucas smothered a smile. He hadn't missed the fact she wasn't wearing a bra. Anytime she was in air conditioning, her nipples puckered, forming twin points against the fabric of her T-shirt.

She lifted her chin, strode up the steps and held out her hand. "Mrs. Crabtree, thank you for contacting me about your floral needs for Colonial Day—and just in time. I was going to place the order today for the flowers I'll need for the event."

The woman briefly laid her hand in Felina's and pulled it away.

Felina turned to Lucas. "I hope you don't mind that I brought my boyfriend, Lucas LeBlanc. He's helping me with the Colonial Day preparations and will work with my usual driver to deliver the arrangements."

Mrs. Crabtree's gaze briefly swept over Lucas. "I suppose it's only natural to want him with you after last night's break-in."

Felina nodded. "Yes, ma'am."

"Does the sheriff have any idea who might have done it?"

"Not yet," Felina said. "They dusted for prints. Hopefully, they'll get a match."

"Since you're here today, I assume he didn't hurt you," the older woman said.

"No, he didn't," Felina said. "Thank you for your concern."

"Fortunate," Mrs. Crabtree said. "Did he take anything?"

Felina snorted softly. "If he did, he didn't get much. I don't have anything of value in my apartment. The only things of value I own are in my shop, wrapped up in the computer and electronics I use to run my business. Thankfully, he didn't get any of that."

"I understand that wasn't the only excitement you had last night," the woman arched an eyebrow. "Wasn't there an altercation at the Crawdad Hole as well?"

Felina blinked. "Yes, ma'am. You're well-informed."

"I have to be. After losing my dear husband recently, I make it my business to be completely aware of what's happening around me. You can never be too cautious. My Thomas is proof of that."

"I'm so sorry for your loss," Felina said. "It was a shock to all of Bayou Mambaloa when we heard of his murder in New Orleans."

"He never should've been there during Mardi Gras. With so many people crowding the streets, anyone could get away with murder and never be caught. My husband is just another of those statistics. It's been six months, and the New Orleans Police still haven't identified a suspect and likely never will."

"I'm sorry to hear that," Felina said. "He will be missed at Colonial Day. He always entertained the guests, pretending to be his great-great-grandfather, talking about how he'd cleared the land and built Crabtree Mansion back in the early eighteen hundreds."

"I almost didn't agree to include Crabtree Mansion in this year's Colonial Day, but I changed my mind. This will, however, be the last one in which I will participate."

Felina's eyebrows rose. "Oh, really? Why?"

"I'm selling the estate." Mrs. Crabtree's gaze swept out across the lawn. "Too many memories in this old house and Bayou Mambaloa. I'm moving to Atlanta next month." She gave Felina a tight smile. "So, you see, I need Crabtree Mansion to look its finest. I've engaged a photographer to take photographs after it's decorated for Colonial Day before guests arrive, and I've contracted with a broker to handle the listing and sale."

Felina nodded. "I understand. I'll do my very best to help make your home picture-perfect. Now, what did you have in mind?"

Lucas stood back while Mrs. Crabtree worked with Felina, discussing potted plants and hanging ferns for the porch. When they moved inside, he followed, taking in the magnificent entryway with its marble floors and sweeping staircase.

Felina dictated notes onto her cell phone as the women discussed what flowers to use and where they would be placed in the foyer, a sitting room, the master bedroom and several of the guest bedrooms.

An hour later, Felina thanked Mrs. Crabtree, promising to get back to her with a quote by the end of the day.

Lucas held the passenger door for Felina as she climbed into the cab.

She waited to say anything until they had left the Crabtree estate. Then she turned toward Lucas, her eyes shining. "Not only will this be a major order, but it will also be showcased in a broker's catalog." Felina shoved a hand through her strawberry-blond hair. "Between Trish's wedding, and now, four homes I'm doing for Colonial Day, I'll be swamped."

"Can you handle it all on your own?" Lucas asked. "I can help, but I'm not skilled in arranging flowers."

Felina tapped a finger to her chin. "My friends have helped in the past. I can tap on them for this surge. Most of the year, I can handle the load by myself. Bayou Mambaloa isn't big enough that my business can grow significantly enough to warrant another full-time employee." She shrugged. "I'll just have to pull some all-nighters for a few days."

Felina sat in the passenger seat, staring out the window, a smile playing on her lips.

Lucas could imagine she was already going through the lists of arrangements, tallying the supplies and flowers she'd have to order. Her eyes sparkled at the challenge.

"You love this, don't you?" he commented, his heart warming at the happiness on her face.

"I do." She shot him a big smile. "I love flowers and how they make people happy."

"How did you get into this business?"

"When I was a little girl, my grandmother lost her eyesight and couldn't live alone, so my parents took her in. It worked out well for all of us since my father worked on the oil rigs and was gone for long periods.

"Grandma helped as much as she could in the house, but she loved working in the garden the most. Though she couldn't see, she could feel and smell. I'd help her in the spring, cleaning out the flower beds and trimming back dead branches. We'd pick peonies in the spring, roses and gardenias in the summer and fill the house with them."

Felina smiled at the memory. "I'd close my eyes and pretend I was blind like my grandmother so I could 'see' what she did with her sense of smell and touch. I didn't have to see the flowers to know they were beautiful. Their petals were so soft, and the smell..." She sighed. "They brought so much joy."

The sweet smile on Felina's face made Lucas's

chest tighten. She was beautiful no matter what, but that smile made her glow with a light that transcended physical beauty.

Lucas wanted her to keep smiling like that. He wanted to be the person who made her that happy.

Felina's smile faded. "When grandma passed, I picked flowers from her garden and arranged them on her grave. I was sad, but the flowers reminded me of the happiness she brought to my life. I think it was at that point in my life that I knew I wanted to work with flowers and bring happiness to others through their beauty."

"How old were you?" Lucas asked.

"Ten," she said. "My father passed away the next year." She looked down at her hands. "It was a dark time for me and my mother. To have lost my grandmother and my father within a year of each other...it was hard. Mom took it the hardest. I had to grow up fast to keep our remaining family of two afloat."

Lucas reached for her hand and squeezed it gently. "That's a lot for an eleven-year-old to handle."

She shrugged. "We survived. After school, I worked for the ladies who used to own the only flower shop in Bayou Mambaloa. I'd sweep, mop and help sort through inventory. The former owners, Ms. Margie and Ms. Martha, let me watch them make beautiful arrangements. Soon, I was making them as well as they were. When I finished high school, I went to community college for a year but came home when Ms. Martha fell ill with cancer. Ms. Margie hired me full-time to run the flower shop while she stayed by Ms. Martha's side through her treatments."

Felina stared out the side window.

Lucas could see the sadness in her reflection in the glass. He knew what losing people you loved and cared about was like. He'd lost teammates in fire-fights. He'd held his battle buddy in his arms as he'd bled out from a fatal wound received from an IED explosion. The pain had eased over time, but he'd never forgotten the love.

"Unfortunately, the cancer won," Felina continued softly. "When Ms. Martha passed, Ms. Margie didn't have the heart to return to the flower shop without her dear friend and partner. Ms. Margie sold the shop to me for a ridiculously low amount that I was able to pay off in a year. I did the flowers for Ms. Martha's funeral and every funeral in Bayou Mambaloa since." Her lips twisted. "Including Mr. Crabtree's."

Lucas frowned. "How was Mr. Crabtree murdered?"

"He was stabbed during a Mardi Gras parade," Felina said, "surrounded by thousands of people, and yet no one saw it happen. They didn't realize he was dead until the crowd started to clear. Most people assumed he was a drunk who'd passed out on the street until a police officer came to rouse him, checked for a pulse and discovered he'd been stabbed in the chest."

"That's harsh," Lucas said.

"Mrs. Crabtree was shocked. Her husband wasn't even supposed to be in New Orleans. He'd told her he was going to some historical society convention in Baton Rouge that weekend."

"He was in the wrong place at the wrong time." Lucas shook his head.

"Yeah. His funeral was lovely. He'd been such a part of the reenactment community in the parish that many of his friends showed up in period costumes as part of his send-off."

As Lucas parked in front of the flower shop next to a cherry-red Mustang convertible, Felina grimaced. "So much for getting to eat lunch. Trish is early for our one o'clock meeting."

The door opened on the convertible. Felina's friend, Trish, stepped out, wearing a pale pink mini skirt with a matching sleeveless shirt. Her sleek, sable-brown hair was pulled back in a tight ponytail, emphasizing high cheekbones and luminous brown eyes.

The woman was stunning. Lucas could see where some men would fall for her looks.

Lucas, however, preferred strawberry blondes with moss-green eyes. Scratch that. He preferred one strawberry blonde with moss-green eyes. He hurried around the truck to help his fake girlfriend out of his truck by grabbing her around the waist and lifting her down, holding on a little longer than was physically necessary.

His protective instincts on alert, he wasn't quite sure how to defend Felina from this threat, whom Felina called a friend.

Lucas brushed a quick kiss across Felina's lips and slipped an arm around her waist before turning to face her boyfriend-stealing sorry-excuse-for-a-best-friend.

CHAPTER 7

"You two are so cute together," Trish said with a smile. "Why did I not know about this love match before last night?"

Felina leaned into Lucas, liking the feel of his arm around her. Warm and strong. "We've both been so busy we haven't had time to talk."

"No kidding. But apparently not too busy on your part," she winked. "I'm so glad you've found your soulmate. It's such a relief to be out of the dating scene. There are so many liars and cheaters out there, it makes you give up hope."

Felina bit down hard on her lip to keep from pointing out that Marty had been one of those liars and cheaters.

Lucas reached into the truck and retrieved the now-cold platters of food. "We were just about to eat our lunch." He held up the bag.

"Oh, don't let me keep you from eating. I had a late breakfast and cleared my schedule until later this afternoon when I have to do highlights and a cut for Aurelie Anderson. She wanted to look fresh and sophisticated for one of her father's political events."

Felina led the way to the front door of her flower shop and inserted the key. "Is she still campaigning with her father?"

"She is. Since her mother's death, she's been at her father's side."

Felina opened the door.

Lucas stepped inside and held the door for the ladies.

"I thought she didn't want to go into politics." Felina moved back for her friend to enter first.

Trish walked through the door with a quick smile for Lucas. "She doesn't, but with her mother's death in the middle of her father's campaign, his campaign strategists thought it better if she stood at his side, showing support."

After Felina entered the shop, Lucas released his hold on the door and let it swing shut.

"That's selfless of her to put her life on hold." Felina flipped the sign on the door to OPEN. "I need to call her. It's been a while since we've had a good long chat or met for a drink at the Crawdad Hole."

"I'd love that. I only see her when she needs her hair done," Trish said.

Lucas led the way to the back workroom, on alert

for intruders. The room was exactly as they'd left it. He set the bag of food on a worktable and pulled the plastic platters out.

Felina took one of the plates, inserted it into a microwave oven in the corner and set it for one minute. "I'm sure she'll be glad when November rolls around and the voting is tallied."

"I'm sure." Trish roamed the room, sniffing the roses and running her fingers across the blooms. "You go ahead and eat. I just wanted to run some ideas by you now that I've had a second look at the venue and a chance to think about what will work on my budget."

The microwave dinged. "I'm listening," Felina said as she pulled the plate out and inserted the next one.

"I'm not going to have the arch of flowers and greenery as originally planned. This whole wedding is costing too much. I'd rather not go into debt for one day when I'll have the rest of my life with Marty." She shot a quick smile at Felina.

Trish's casual comment about spending the rest of her life with Felina's old boyfriend barely fazed Felina. She really didn't care that Trish was marrying Marty. Her biggest beef with the situation was that they'd gone behind her back. Marty should have ended things with her before starting something with Trish.

"I thought you had money saved for the wedding." Felina peeled the cover off the heated plate, set it on the table and nodded toward Lucas. "Go ahead while it's hot."

"I did have a little money saved, but things...came up, and I had to use it. So, rather than charge up my credit cards any more than they already are, I'm cutting back on some of the wedding plans. I'm not having a dinner. We'll have finger foods at the reception. That's going to save me tons. And instead of a band, I got my cousin Arty, the DJ, to provide the music for the wedding and reception. I just have to give him gas money."

Felina frowned. "These are some pretty drastic changes with the event only two weeks out. Is everything okay?"

Trish gave her a too-bright smile. "Yes. Of course. I just don't want to burden Marty and our marriage with any more debt than I have to."

"The things that came up..." Felina stared at Trish, "are they things I can help with?"

Trish shook her head. "No. I'm the only one who can take care of them. I don't think they'll be a problem anymore, and I have a plan to pay off my debt." She flashed a smile. "The plan involves a lot of hair appointments. So, are you okay with backing off the floral arch and maybe making a simpler bouquet? And we won't need the table decorations since we're not doing a sit-down dinner."

"I'm still doing the original bouquet," Felina said. "It'll be my gift to you. And let me take a second look at the pavilion where you're having the ceremony. I might have some less expensive ideas we can employ other than flowers."

"When do you want to meet at the pavilion?" Trish asked.

"I can be there after five if that works for you," Felina offered.

Trish closed her eyes for a moment. "I think it will. My last appointment is at four, and it's just a cut and style. I can meet you at the pavilion. Then we can go to the community center where we're holding the reception."

"Sounds good." Felina smiled. "Don't worry. Your wedding would be beautiful even if you showed up in a gunny sack. You're going to be a gorgeous bride. Marty won't be able to take his eyes off you for a second."

Trish's eyes pooled. "You think so?"

"I know so," Felina said.

Trish crossed the room and threw her arms around Felina. "You're too good to me. I really don't deserve your friendship."

Felina hugged Trish back. "It all works out. I just got a big job for Colonial Day. With you downsizing the floral decorations at your wedding, I can focus on the new job."

"Perfect," Trish said, brushing a hand across her cheek. "You've made such a success of your business. I'm so proud of you and thankful you're still my friend."

111

Her friend squared her shoulders and gave Felina a nod. "Now, I've got to get back to those haircuts and high-lights. I have a wedding to pay for. I'll see you at five."

Trish left the building.

"You're a better person than I am," Lucas murmured.

"Why?" Felina lifted the sliced brisket sandwich off the plate and sank her teeth into it.

"Most women wouldn't talk to the person who broke up their relationship."

Felina finished chewing and swallowed. "Trish doesn't mean anyone harm. I choose to think she recognized that Marty and I had drifted apart. Besides, we've been friends since grade school. I never had a sibling. She's the closest I've ever come to having a sister. I'm not losing her over a man."

"No siblings?" Lucas asked.

"I'm the only one," she said. "And if I ever have children, it will be more than one. Only children never really get the full effect of childhood. I want my children to have someone to confide in, a built-in friend." She stared across her sandwich at him. "Do you have brothers or sisters?"

Lucas nodded. "I have two sisters and one brother. Our home was always loud and rowdy." He grinned at the memories. "We had our share of fights, but we had each other's backs. I wouldn't trade my childhood or any of my siblings for anything."

"You're lucky," Felina said softly. "I envied families like yours." She took a few more bites of her sandwich and then wrapped it up and put it in the refrigerator. "I have to get some work done before I meet Trish at the pavilion."

"I can get a start on cleaning up the apartment. Besides the glass on the floor, the dust they used to lift prints will need to be washed away." Lucas frowned. "Only I don't like the idea of leaving you alone down here."

Her heart warmed at his concern. Granted, it was his job, and he was obligated to be concerned. But it still felt good that someone cared enough to worry about her. Marty never had.

Felina touched his arm. "I'll be all right. No one's going to attack me in broad daylight."

Lucas's frown deepened. "Are you willing to bank your life on that assumption?"

It was Felina's turn to frown. "You think they'll come during the daytime?"

"Since we don't know who they are, it's hard to guess," Lucas said. "Tell you what. I'll leave the door open and check on you often. If anyone threatens you, all you have to do is yell, and I'll come running. What do you say?"

"I'd say you're overcompensating for a situation that isn't likely to happen." Her lips twisted. "But after having an intruder break into my apartment—

something I never thought would happen to me—I say your idea sounds like a winner."

At that moment, a voice from the front reception area called, "Hello? Anyone home?"

Lucas and Felina hurried to see who was calling out.

A man wearing jeans, a blue denim work shirt and a leather tool belt with a hammer, several screwdrivers, a pencil and a tape measure stood among the displays of flowers.

"Richard." Felina hurried forward and hugged her favorite carpenter. "Thank you for coming so soon."

"Hey, Felina." He hugged her tightly, lifting her off the ground. "How's my second favorite woman in the whole world?"

She laughed as he set her on the ground. "You'd better not let Lacy hear you flirting with me."

"Lacy knows I love you. I told her that if she ever decides to leave me, I'd marry you next."

Felina crossed her arms over her chest. "And do I have a say in that plan?"

"Of course not. I can't let logic play a part in this scenario. I'd lose." Richard held out a hand to Lucas. "You must be Lucas. It's a pleasure to meet you. Are you the man who stole the heart of Bayou Mambaloa's favorite florist?"

Lucas nodded. "That would be me, the heart stealer." He winked at Felina and took Richard's hand in a tight grip.

"Yeah, well, hopefully, you won't hurt her. We look out for our own around here."

Lucas's eyes widened and quickly narrowed as he shook Richard's hand, his lips pressing together in a line. "I have no intention of hurting Ms. Faivre," he said through gritted teeth.

The handshake went on longer than Felina would have expected, neither man relinquishing his hold, their knuckles turning white.

What was this, some kind of male domination contest? What were they trying to prove?

"Seriously?" Felina frowned and crossed her arms over her chest. "Cut it out."

The two men released their grips at once, shaking blood back into their hands.

"Just wanted to make sure your man has your best interests at heart," Richard said. "Unlike Marty."

"Like you have time for male posturing," she said. "You have a lot to do to get a new door installed by the end of the day."

"That's right," Lucas said.

Felina turned to Lucas. "And you promised to clean up the mess in my apartment. Standing around in a pissing contest isn't accomplishing anything."

"On it," Lucas tipped his head toward the stairs leading up to the apartment, a crooked smile lifting the corners of his lips. "Come on. I'll show you where to start."

"Good." Richard followed Lucas up the stairs. "If

the door I brought fits, I could use a hand carrying it up."

"No worries," Lucas was saying as he opened the door to Felina's apartment. "I have some basic carpentry skills. Any way I can help, let me know."

"You're on." Richard entered Felina's apartment after Lucas.

Felina shook her head. What was it with men thinking they had to protect her all the time? Richard was married to one of Felina's friends. She'd known Lacy and Richard all her life. They'd all grown up in Bayou Mambaloa. Hell, they were family. And, as family, Richard was only looking out for her.

For the most part, Felina loved living in a small town where people looked out for each other. When they tried to decide who Felina should date or marry, it got to be a little too much.

The bell over the front entrance rang, alerting Felina that someone had come inside. She hurried to see who it was.

Missy Thornbridge transferred her white, designer purse from one arm to the other and smoothed a hand over her sleek, powder-gray skirt. Her striking white hair was pulled back from her face and secured in a perfect twist at the back of her head. She removed her sunglasses and smiled. "Ah, Felina. I'm glad I caught you."

"Mrs. Thornbridge, it's nice to see you," Felina said with a smile, once again wishing she had taken the time to find suitable clothes for greeting customers. The jeans she'd worn to the bar the night before with the ripped knee made her feel like a kid from the wrong side of the tracks.

Which wasn't too far off the truth, but still. She'd have felt a lot more confident dressed in clean, professional clothes and a bra.

Now that she could get into her apartment, she'd remedy her clothing situation as soon as she dealt with Missy. "What can I do for you?"

Missy drifted around the small reception area, studying the silk flowers and the fresh arrangements behind the glass doors of the refrigerator. "I was in town getting my nails done and thought I'd stop by."

Felina hid a smile. Missy was one of Bayou Mambaloa's most notorious gossips. That fact, coupled with a trip to the nail salon, meant she'd heard something juicy and was looking for more information. The woman's next words confirmed half of Felina's supposition.

"I heard Brenda Crabtree is opening Crabtree Mansion for Colonial Day." She turned to fully face Felina. "And that she asked you to provide the floral displays for the event."

Felina nodded. "She is, and I am." She cocked an eyebrow.

"Will you be able to handle her order as well as mine? I mean, will it be too much work for one person to manage?" She touched Felina's arm. "I wouldn't want you to be overworked or unable to finish everything on time."

"Don't worry, Mrs. Thornbridge, I know my capabilities. I provided florals for Colonial Day last year for five participating estates."

"Yes, yes, of course." Missy switched her purse to the other arm. "I'm just concerned about everything being done in time for opening day. After all, I put my order in months ago."

"Yes, ma'am. It's on the books," Felina smiled reassuringly. "I'll have everything completed and delivered the morning of opening day."

"Good. I just got nervous that you would be overwhelmed." Missy frowned. "None of us thought she'd open Crabtree Mansion for Colonial Day since her husband's passing. He was the one who insisted on participating." She shook her head. "Thomas was so passionate about his heritage. It was too bad that wasn't the only thing he was passionate about."

Felina had things to do besides listen to Missy's gossip. However, she reminded herself that this woman gave her a lot of business. Not only the large order she'd made for Colonial Day but throughout the year. She liked fresh flower arrangements in her home for every dinner party, soiree and tea she hosted. So, Felina listened politely, praying she'd get to the point and leave soon.

"I never thought Brenda would give a damn about carrying on the Crabtree tradition after Thomas's

flagrant disregard for the sanctity of their marriage."
Missy's mouth twisted disapprovingly. "I would've
left him long ago had he been my husband." She
touched a finger to a silk rose. "But then, she didn't
have a choice, what with the prenup he made her
sign." The older woman snorted softly. "Can't say that
I blame Thomas for doing that. He loved his family
home. It had been in his family for two hundred
years. How horrible would it have been to lose it in a
divorce?"

"Pretty bad," Felina said, though Thomas wouldn't
have had to worry if he hadn't been cheating on his
wife.

"Anyway," Missy paused, "I came to see if I could
alter my order just a teensy bit."

Finally. The point.

"Certainly," Felina said. "I'm placing my order this
afternoon. We can make changes up until I place the
order." She turned to grab a pen and paper from
behind the counter. "What exactly would you like to
change?"

"I'd like the display for the front entryway to be
bigger. Add at least two dozen more roses. And, if
it's not too much to ask, I'd like to double the
number of hanging ferns and add a floral display to
be placed in front of the fireplace in the sitting
room. I'll give you carte blanche to make certain
Thornbridge Manor shines above all others for this
year's Colonial Day." She waved a hand with all the

drama of a rich plantation owner. "Money is no object."

"Yes, ma'am," Felina said. "I'll keep that in mind."

"Perfect," Missy said. "I'm glad you understand. Now, I'm off to play bridge."

"Have a lovely day, Mrs. Thornbridge," Felina said.

"I will." The older woman breezed out the door without looking back.

Felina shook her head.

"What was that all about?" a voice said behind her.

Felina turned to find Lucas stepping out of the shadows between the workroom and the reception area.

Felina grinned. "That was Missy Thornbridge stopping by to make sure her floral displays are bigger and better than anyone else's for Colonial Day." She narrowed her eyes. "How long have you been standing there?"

"Since shortly after I heard the bell over the door ring."

"You heard it all the way up in my apartment?"

"I did. However, once your carpenter starts hammering, I won't be able to hear anything. I'll come down and hang out with you." He looked out the window. "If you're okay for the moment, I'll see how much I can get done before Richard brings all his tools up."

"I'm fine." Felina ripped the page of notes she'd

taken off the pad. "I'll be in the workroom on my computer for much of the afternoon. Today's the day I place orders for Colonial Day and Trish's wedding. That'll take some time."

Lucas followed her into the workroom. "Is Missy always so free with gossip?"

Felina laughed. "Always. Although we all assumed Thomas Thornbridge wasn't at Mardi Gras alone, I didn't know he'd made his wife sign a pre-nuptial agreement." Felina shrugged. "It makes sense to protect your assets when you're that rich. But sadly, none of that matters now since he passed away. His wife has everything anyway."

Lucas frowned. "I'd think she would've been the prime suspect."

"Oh, she was," Felina said. "But she had an alibi. She was home when her husband was murdered. Her gardener verified that she was there all day, and her car never left the garage. Plus, she hosted a bridge game later that afternoon. The sheriff delivered the news of her husband's death in the middle of the game."

The bell over the front door rang.

Felina and Lucas moved as one toward the reception area.

A tall man with black hair and blue eyes let the door close behind him and smiled at Felina and Lucas. Felina recognized him as Remy Montagne, Shelby's fiancé.

Lucas hurried forward, his hand held out. "Remy, what brings you by?"

He shook Lucas's hand and nodded toward Felina. "I was hoping to catch you two. Shelby asked me to stop by and let you know they've identified the man they found in the bayou."

Felina's heart skipped several beats. "Who is he?"

Remy met her gaze. "Willard Gaither. Does that name ring any bells?"

She shook her head. "Not even one."

"He was a private investigator out of New Orleans."

"Private investigator? Who was he investigating?" Felina asked.

Remy shook his head. "We don't know that yet. It might take time to get access to his files."

"Someone obviously didn't like being investigated," Lucas said.

Felina frowned. "Or what he found."

CHAPTER 8

LUCAS PACED SEVERAL STEPS AWAY, digesting Remy's announcement. "I'm struggling to find a connection between Gaither's death and Felina's break-in."

"They could be two completely separate incidents," Remy offered.

"My gut's telling me they're connected," Lucas said.

"Why would this Gaither dude be investigating me?" Felina asked. "My life is an open book. I have no secrets."

"If he wasn't investigating you," Remy said, "then who would he have been following that would make someone believe you're involved?"

"I saw the guy who threw Gaither into the SUV. That has to be the reason they targeted me." Her brow twisted. "Though they didn't really come after me, or they would have found me. They were looking for something in my apartment. I don't have anything anyone would want."

Lucas stared at Felina, his eyes narrowing. "When I found you behind the bar, you said the guy who pushed you felt you up." He tilted his head. "By felt you up, what exactly did you mean?"

"I don't know," she said. "It happened so fast." She turned her head from side to side.

"Close your eyes, Felina," Lucas urged gently. "Talk us through what happened from the moment you stepped out the back door to when I found you."

"I told you everything," she said.

"Humor me," he said.

She sighed. "Fine. I have a million and one things to do, but for you, I'll close my eyes and tell you what I told you before."

Felina closed her eyes. "I told you I needed to go to the bathroom. When I entered the hallway to the bathroom, I spotted the exit sign at the end. Instead of stopping at the ladies' room, I pushed through the back exit out onto the landing."

While she spoke, Lucas crept around behind her.

"I was standing there, debating walking back to my apartment or going back inside and asking Bernie to drive me home when the door burst open.

"A man ran into me from behind. We both almost fell off the stoop. He wrapped his arms around me until we both got our balance back. Then he stuck his hand in my pocket."

"Like this?" Lucas slid his hand into her back pocket, shocked when he felt something there. He pulled it out and grinned when he realized it was a condom.

"No," Felina said. "It was a lot more personal. He put his hand in my front pocket. I was so shocked. Before I could defend myself, he shoved me off the landing."

"He slid his hand into which pocket?" Lucas asked, his hands lowering to rest on her hips.

Felina leaned her back into him. "I don't remember," she said breathily.

"Was it the left pocket?" He slid one hand into her left pocket. It was empty.

She shook her head, her breath catching. "No, not the left."

Lucas slid his other hand into her right pocket.

"Yes," she whispered. "That's the pocket."

The right pocket was empty as well. Lucas dragged his hands out, his thoughts churning.

"Headlights flashed at the other end of the parking area. Then he shoved me off the landing and leaped over me. The SUV drove up, a big man got out, grabbed Gaither, shoved him into the back seat and they drove off. That's when you found me." Felina opened her eyes and turned around.

"Could he have slipped something into your pocket?" Lucas asked.

"I would have felt it if he had."

"Unless it was soft or small," Lucas stared at her jeans. "Where were you when you took off the jeans?"

"In my apartment," she said. "I took them off in the bathroom and left them on the floor."

Lucas spun and headed for the stairs.

Remy followed. "What are you thinking?"

"Yeah, clue me in, will ya?" Felina hurried after the two men as they climbed the stairs to her apartment.

Richard was hard at work with a crowbar, pulling the trim away from the doorframe.

Lucas went straight to the bathroom. He remembered grabbing the jeans off the floor when he'd gone through her apartment, gathering a few things she might need until the latent print expert could get there to dust for fingerprints.

He bent low and searched the bathroom floor.

Felina squatted next to him. "What are we looking for?"

"I don't know. Something small you might not have felt in your pocket. It could've fallen out when you took off your jeans." Lucas lifted a towel off the floor, raised the bathmat and checked behind the toilet and found nothing.

He straightened and looked around the mess in the room. "Why would Gaither slide his hand into your pocket one second and shove you off the landing a moment later?"

"Do you think the headlights flashing scared him,

and he shoved Felina in a knee-jerk reaction?" Remy suggested.

"Maybe," Lucas said as he mentally retraced his steps in relation to the jeans Felina was wearing. "You didn't take off the jeans in the bedroom and drop them in the bathroom?"

Felina shook her head. "No. They were exactly where I left them when you picked them up and shoved them into the pillowcase with my pillow."

"The pillowcase," he murmured and headed for the stairs leading into the shop. At the bottom of the stairs, he looked around. "Where did you put the pillow and blanket?"

"In the bathroom on the supply shelf," Felina said, descending the stairs behind him. "Along with the other items you stuffed in it."

He entered the bathroom, took the pillow down and pulled the pillow out of the case.

"Nothing."

"Last night, I dumped the contents of the pillow-case onto the sleeping bag," Felina reminded him.

"And shook the bag out this morning before I rolled it up and stashed it in the corner." Lucas stared at the floor, littered with stems, leaves, bits of ribbon and pieces of Styrofoam bases.

"I guess now is as good a time as any to clean up after my mad dash to get things done this morning," she said.

Felina pulled the broom and dustpan out of the

bathroom and went to work, sweeping everything into a pile in the center of the floor.

While Lucas and Remy sifted through the pile, she bent low and swept beneath the workbenches lining the walls, moving buckets of flowers aside one at a time.

When she moved the bucket full of yellow roses, she found a tiny square piece of plastic. She bent to pick it up. It was smaller than a micro-SD card used in some cameras and reminded her of the SIM cards used in cell phones. "Here's something that doesn't belong to me. Is this what I think it is?" She turned toward the two men brushing dust off their hands.

Remy reached for the card. "It's a nano card."

"Like the ones used in cell phones?" she asked.

"Yes, among other things," Lucas leaned over Remy's hand. "And it's small enough you might not have felt it in your pocket."

"Holy hell." Felina's face drained of color. "Do you think it contains information people would kill for?"

"I don't know," Lucas said. "But we're sure as hell going to find out." He crossed to her computer and studied its ports. "We're going to need a special device to read this card."

"Let me take it to the boat factory," Remy said. "Swede and Hank equipped us with just about every electronic device we could possibly use."

Felina's brow wrinkled. "At the boat factory? I thought they were making boats there again."

"We are," Remy said. "At least on the surface for the casual observer. We've created a southern regional headquarters of the Brotherhood Protectors."

"We're the Bayou Brotherhood Protectors," Lucas said. "Come on, let's get that card to the boat factory."

"Shouldn't we take it straight to the sheriff's office?" Felina asked. "What if it contains evidence that could be used to solve Gaither's murder?"

"We absolutely will hand it over to the sheriff's department," Remy said, "as soon as we see what's on it. It might not have belonged to Gaither."

"Then how did it get into my shop?"

"It could've come in with a batch of your flowers," Lucas said. "In which case, we'd be wasting the sheriff's time."

Felina's lips pressed together. "It's a weak excuse."

"But one I could live with," Remy said.

"If we hand it over to the sheriff's office, they'll probably send it off to the state to access what's on it. Who knows how long that would take? If this contains information that could lead to those responsible for Gaither's murder, it might also lead us to the people who ransacked your apartment." Lucas brushed his finger along her cheek and lowered his voice. "I'd like to know that information sooner rather than later."

Felina turned to Remy. "Won't Shelby be mad at you?"

"Better to ask forgiveness than permission," Remy said. "But I think she'd agree that state would take too long, though she'd never admit it out loud." He glanced at Lucas. "I'll head that way and see what I need to do to download what's on the disk."

"We're right behind you," Lucas called out as Remy left the shop with the disk in his pocket. Lucas turned to Felina and held out his hand. "Are you ready?"

She grimaced. "I was supposed to spend the afternoon getting my orders in for Colonial Day and the wedding. I'm running short on time." Felina stared around her workroom, frowning.

Lucas waited, his hand extended.

With a sigh, Felina placed her hand in his palm. "What the hell? It's all online. I can put in my orders at midnight if I have to. Let's see what's on that disk."

Lucas grinned. "I'll stay up with you. We can order pizza and play '80s music."

Felina's brow twisted. "Why '80s music?"

"Because I like it." He raised her hand to his lips. "I'll let your carpenter know we'll be back later. Hopefully, before he leaves."

"I hate closing the shop. I have several customers who are supposed to come by to pick up their orders after they get off work."

"Text them and let them know you'll be back by four-thirty. I'll make sure you are."

"Give me a few minutes to look up their information," she said.

While she pulled up her customers' numbers, Lucas ran up the stairs to her apartment and let Richard know they were leaving for a while.

"Before you go, could you help me carry the door up the stairs and set it into the frame?" Richard asked. "It won't take long. I've already measured. It'll fit."

"Sure."

The two men walked down the outside stairs, unloaded the heavy metal door from Richard's truck and carried it up the stairs. After a few minutes, they had the door moved into position.

"I can take it from here," Richard said. "If you're not back by the time I finish, I'll lock up and leave the keys to the door on the kitchen table."

"Great," Lucas said. "Thanks. Felina will be happy to have a functioning door that can't be broken."

Richard shook his head. "Scary times when you don't feel safe in your own place."

"Tell me about it." Lucas shook the man's hand. "Thank you for fortifying Felina's apartment."

"Happy to do it. All kidding aside, she's a great person. The wife and I love her and don't want anything bad to happen to her. She might not be a blood relative, but she's family."

Lucas hurried back to Felina's workroom. He

knew Felina was special. It warmed his heart that others felt the same.

"All set," she said, looping her purse strap over her shoulder. "I just need to be back by four-thirty so they can pick up their orders."

"We'll make it happen." Lucas rested a hand on the small of her back as they passed through the shop and out the front door, only pausing long enough to switch the sign around to CLOSED and lock up.

The drive to the boat factory didn't take long. Lucas pulled into the newly paved parking lot and shifted into park.

Felina stared at the building, shaking her head. "I haven't been out here since they finished the remodel of the old factory. Wow. It looks modern and chic. And you can really make boats inside?"

Lucas laughed. "Nothing fancy, just aluminum skiffs. Hank invested in new metal fabrication equipment and the technology to automate much of the work. He liked the idea of maintaining the building's heritage. But the heart of the building is the Bayou Brotherhood Protectors war room and offices."

He led her through the boat factory and paused at a door where he pressed his finger to a pad and scanned his eye in a biometric reader. The lock clicked, and the door swung open into a hallway that lit up as they moved through it, passing several doors along the way.

"Behind these doors are storerooms containing

electronics, body armor and communications equipment, as well as an armory equipped with an array of weapons we might need for whatever mission we're assigned."

"Are you anticipating a war like the preppers up in the northeast?" Felina asked.

"Not necessarily," Lucas said. "The Brotherhood Protectors have been known to deploy to hostile locations in other countries as well as here in our homeland. Having the right equipment on hand allows us to mobilize on short notice."

"I didn't realize all of this was here or that your team could perform such a wide variety of missions. I guess I thought you were just a security firm that provided bodyguards for celebrities or politicians."

Lucas grinned. "We've done that, too. Hank hires former military guys who are highly trained in special operations. We have skills most civilians don't."

"I feel guilty that I hired you for such a silly assignment. Pretending to be my boyfriend to get the matchmakers off my back seems like a waste of your skills."

Lucas shook his head. "We're still not tasked at full capacity. Besides, no assignment is too big or too small. I think we've hired out as security for a kid's birthday party at the same time as we've stormed a compound up north that was kidnapping people and training them as assassins."

"Seriously?" Felina stared up at him. "Okay, I definitely feel bad for hiring you to be my boyfriend."

"Don't feel bad. It turns out you needed more than a pretend boyfriend. With a murderer on the loose and the break-in, having a protector isn't a bad idea."

They emerged from the hallway into a large room with a conference table in the middle, a large video monitor at the end of the table, a wall of whiteboards and a bank of computers and monitors.

Remy stood behind a man with broad shoulders and sandy-blond hair who sat in front of an array of monitors, his hands on a keyboard.

As Lucas and Felina approached, Remy glanced up. "Fortunately, we had a sleeve-like device we could slip the disk into that fits in a port on the computer. Unfortunately, the disk is password protected." He nodded to the man at the computer. "This is Landry Laurent, former Navy SEAL and the most tech-savvy member of our team here in Louisiana. We have a couple of other computer gurus at other locations we can tap into when we need more technical prowess than we have here. Landry, this is Felina Faivre."

"The flower shop girl." Landry shot a smile over his shoulder. "Our man Lucas has been trying to get your attention since we arrived in Bayou Mambaloa. Nice to meet you."

Lucas's cheeks heated. "Thanks, man."

Landry grinned. "Just the facts, man. Have him show you his room at the boarding house. I've never seen so many flowers in a bachelor pad."

Felina chuckled. "I thought he was buying them for his girlfriend."

"In a way, he was." Landry gave Felina a wink. "Can't knock the man for persistence. Although some women might have mistaken persistence for stalking. Tomato, to-mah-to. Whatever you want to call it, I'm not making much headway on this password."

"What have you tried?" Lucas asked.

"Gaither's birthday in a variety of combinations. His business address in New Orleans—again, in a variety of combinations. His phone number, first name, last name, middle name and combinations of all three. We don't know if he has a pet or what his favorite sports team is or we'd try that. We could be here until we're old and gray and not guess his password. I'm about ready to hand off to Swede, our computer whiz at our main headquarters in Montana."

"Gaither was a private investigator," Felina said. "Who are some famous private investigators?"

"Sherlock Holmes," Remy said.

Landry's fingers flew across the keyboard, trying several combinations of the name. Each time, he got an immediate response of "Invalid Password." Finally, he shook his head.

"How about Hercule Poirot?" Lucas offered.

Landry's brow twisted. "You know Agatha Christie?"

"I love mysteries," Lucas admitted. "Don't judge."

"Let's try it," Landry said and keyed several combinations before saying, "Next."

"The only other famous private investigator I can think of is Nancy Drew." Felina shrugged. "I obviously need to read more mysteries."

Landry keyed in Nancy Drew. The Invalid Password message didn't come up.

For a long moment, the computer churned. A list of files popped up.

"We're in." Landry clicked on the first file.

A photograph popped up on the screen.

Felina, Lucas and Remy leaned closer.

"I'm not sure what we're looking at," Felina said. "Is that a face?" She pointed at the screen.

"Looks like one," Lucas said.

"He looks familiar," Felina's brow furrowed as she stared at the face in a sea of what looked like feathers and sequins. Then she remembered the recent mention of New Orleans. Mr. Crabtree had been murdered in New Orleans.

The more she studied the image, the more convinced she became of who it was. "That's Mr. Crabtree."

"Are you certain?" Remy asked.

"Absolutely," Felina said. "He was in the shop often enough I remember his face. That is his face.

And it appears he's surrounded by people. Are those beaded necklaces?"

"They are," Landry confirmed.

Felina's gaze met Lucas's. "Mardi Gras."

"It appears Gaither was following Mr. Crabtree, snapping pictures," Lucas said. "Who are the people around him?"

Landry leaned close, his brow creased. "Hard to tell who is with him or who is just another face in the crowd."

"Can't see many faces in that crowd," Felina commented. "They're wearing ostrich feather masks that completely cover their faces."

"The one in the blue mask appears to be talking to Mr. Crabtree."

"Pull up the next image," Felina said. "He took quite a few photos. "

Landry clicked on the next file, and an image much like the one before appeared. In this photo, the woman in the blue mask pressed a kiss to Mr. Crabtree's lips.

"What do you want to bet that isn't Mrs. Crabtree?" Lucas muttered. "Next photo."

In this image, the blue-masked woman had turned and walked away, her back to Mr. Crabtree. The man appeared to be calling out to her retreating figure.

"Next," Lucas urged.

The blue-masked woman was gone. On the opposite side from where she'd stood, another woman appeared, wearing a green sequined dress and a green mask. The mask's feathers completely covered her face from forehead to below the chin. Lucas could just make out a hint of red hair. She rested a hand on Mr. Crabtree's shoulder and wore a large emerald ring on her middle finger.

"Next," Lucas said.

Instead of a photo, a short video played, starting with the woman in the blue mask kissing Mr. Crabtree and then the woman in the green mask approaching the man and placing her hand on his shoulder.

He turned toward her, a frown furrowing his brow.

The crowd around them surged, pushing them together in a blur of motion.

Then the woman in green appeared to hug the man, then stepped away, disappearing into the crowd.

Mr. Crabtree stood for a moment, his eyes wide, his mouth forming an O. Then he sank into the sea of faces.

"Oh, sweet Jesus." Felina stiffened beside Lucas. "What's the date on that video? Is there a date?" Her face was pale, her gaze pinned to the screen that had frozen on the last image of the crowd sans Crabtree.

"February third of this year," Landry said.

"What day was Thomas Crabtree murdered?" Lucas asked. "Can you look it up?"

Landry opened another window on the screen and keyed in *Thomas Crabtree murder.*

Several articles mentioned the murder. Landry clicked on one. "He was killed on February third of this year,"

Felina met Lucas's gaze. "This video is of Thomas Crabtree's murder."

CHAPTER 9

"PLAY IT AGAIN," Remy said. "This time, slow it down."

Landry started the video from the beginning and set the speed to half of normal.

Felina focused on the women in the masks.

"There are so many people packing the streets. I don't know how Gaither managed to get these shots," Lucas said.

"He had to be standing on something," Remy commented.

The blue-masked woman said something to Crabtree that made his brow furrow. He shook his head and gripped the woman's arm.

She leaned close, brushed a kiss across Crabtree's cheek and pulled loose of the man's grip.

When he reached for her again, she held up a hand. People bumped into her, surging toward the street to get a closer look at the floats.

Crabtree seemed to be calling out to her.

She shook her head and moved through the throng of parade watchers until she disappeared out of the camera's range.

"Pause the video," Remy said.

Landry hit the pause button.

"Could you note any distinguishable features for the blue woman?" Remy asked. "Any scars, tattoos, eye color?"

"The mask covered her face," Lucas said. "Pale skin. She was almost as tall as Crabtree, though, based on the people around him, he didn't stand out as taller than most. I'd put him at under six feet tall. Maybe five-foot-ten-ish. The woman was a few inches shorter but average to tall for a female."

"She had long, brown hair and a pointy chin," Felina added. "I didn't see any tattoos, and I couldn't see enough of her eyes to tell the color. But, given her brown hair, she probably had dark eyes."

Remy nodded. "Play."

Landry pressed the play button, and the video continued slowly.

Crabtree craned his neck as if searching the crowd for the blue-masked woman. The woman dressed in the green sequined gown and flamboyant green feathered mask came up behind him, insinuating herself through the crowd.

As she neared Crabtree, she placed a hand on his shoulder.

Felina studied the hand and arm, searching for tattoos or scars, neither of which were evident. But she wore an emerald ring on her middle finger that matched her green dress and mask. It was a big square stone set in gold with sparkling diamonds on either side.

Her back was to the camera.

"Reddish-brown shoulder-length hair," Felina said.

"She's shorter and thinner than the other woman," Remy noted.

Crabtree turned toward the woman, a frown pulling his eyebrows low for a moment, then they shot up.

"He looks surprised for just a moment."

"Like maybe he recognizes the woman?"

"Yeah, and then he's frowning again."

Remy pointed at the screen. "Watch her right hand on Crabtree's arm. She slides it down and grips his arm."

"We can't see what's happening with the other hand," Felina said, leaning even closer as if it would help her see between the people crowded around Crabtree and the green-masked woman. It didn't.

"No, we can't, but her body movement tells the story. There," Lucas said, his eyes narrowed. "She stiffens, and her left side pushes forward sharply."

Landry paused the video.

"The police reports said Crabtree was stabbed in the chest."

"Look at his face," Lucas said. "His eyes are wide, surprised."

Landry eased the video forward another second or two.

The green-masked woman said something to Crabtree, then stepped backward, fading into the crowd and out of view of the camera.

Crabtree stood for a moment longer as if suspended in time. Then he slipped below the heads of the crowd around him. At the same time, a float rolled by. People pushed toward the street, stepping or stumbling over the man on the ground without stopping to check on him.

Felina's gut knotted. She'd just witnessed a murder. Seeing it happen in slow motion was even more gut-wrenching than in real-time.

"So, Crabtree was fooling around with a woman or two in New Orleans," Lucas said.

"Appears so," Landry said.

"There's no doubt the woman in green killed him, but was the one in blue in on it?" Remy tilted his head slightly, his eyes narrowing. "Did she distract him so the other woman could slip in for the kill?"

"I can't imagine either one of them hired Gaither to spy on the old man," Felina said.

"No kidding," Lucas said. "They wouldn't have wanted any of what happened documented."

"It leaves them vulnerable for blackmail."

"A private investigator wouldn't waste his time photographing a man unless he was being paid."

"Could he have been following one of the women?" Felina asked.

Remy shook his head. "The PI's camera was on Crabtree the entire time. The women came and went. Crabtree was his target."

Lucas crossed his arms over his chest. "The sixty-four-million-dollar question is who paid Gaither to follow Crabtree?"

"The most logical answer would be Mrs. Crabtree," Remy said. "She has to have suspected he was fooling around and hired Gaither to document it."

"So, she could file for divorce and take him to the cleaners?" Landry asked.

Felina shook her head. "Even if she did have proof of his cheating, she couldn't divorce him without losing everything. From what Missy Thornbridge told me today, Thomas Crabtree made his wife, Brenda, sign a pre-nuptial agreement that states she gets nothing if they divorce."

"All the more reason to murder him."

Remy pulled his cell phone out of his pocket. "Landry, burn a copy of that video, send one to Swede and bring him up on video conference."

"Yes, sir." Landry's fingers flew over the keyboard.

Remy turned away and spoke into his cell phone. "Hey, babe, could you come by the boat factory? We have something you'll want to see. Great. See you in a few."

The big monitor over the conference table blinked to life, and a giant head appeared.

Felina blinked at the white-blond-haired Norseman hovering over them.

"Hey, Swede," Remy turned to Felina. "This is Lucas's mission, Felina Faivre."

Swede dipped his head. "Nice to meet you, Ms. Faivre. Your ex-boyfriend is a fool."

Felina's cheeks heated. "Thanks. Does everyone in the country know I was dumped?"

Swede grinned. "If by everyone, you mean me, then yes."

"And me," another man stepped into view with a little boy in his arms. "I'm Hank Patterson, and this is Axel Svenson. As you might have already guessed, we call him Swede. Bet you can't guess why." Hank glanced down at the dark-haired toddler he held. "And this little stud is McClain Patterson. The boss."

Felina smiled. "Adorable."

"Thanks," Hank said. "My wife thinks so. She thinks the kid is kind of cute, too."

Felina laughed. "Nice to meet you both."

Hank transferred his attention to Remy and Lucas. "Were they able to identify the body?"

Remy and Lucas nodded.

"Willard Gaither, a private investigator out of New Orleans."

"Interesting." Hank's brow twisted. "Do they know why he was in Bayou Mambaloa last night?"

"We were all wondering that very thing." Remy glanced toward Felina. "When he shoved Felina last night, he slipped a nanodisc into her pocket. She didn't find it until this afternoon."

"Why would he do that?" Hank asked.

"Considering he turned up dead this morning, we can only guess he didn't want whoever killed him to have it."

Hank frowned. "What was on the disk?"

"We sent a video to Swede," Lucas said.

Hank bent over Swede's shoulder as the Viking worked his keyboard. Then they both grew still, brows furrowing. Then Hank and Swede's eyes widened.

"Did she just do what I think she did?" Hank asked.

"Kill that man?" Remy's mouth pressed into a thin line. "That's our hypothesis. Given the date on the clip, it coincides with the death of a local, Thomas Crabtree, six months ago. Felina confirmed the man in the video was Thomas Crabtree."

Hank glanced up. "And the women?"

Remy and Lucas shook their heads.

"At this moment, we don't know who they are," Remy said.

"And the PI had this video?" Hank shook his head. "You say Crabtree was killed six months ago? Is this the first anyone's seen of this?"

"That we know of," Remy said. "Shelby's on her way here."

"Not on her way..." a voice called out from across the room, "here."

Remy turned with a smile and held out his hand. "Hey."

"Hey, yourself." Shelby crossed to take his hand in hers, then looked around at the people gathered. She dipped her head toward Felina. "Hi, Hank. Swede. What's the occasion?"

"Our dead man left a present for Felina." Remy nodded toward the computer screen in front of Landry.

"Before or after his untimely death?" Shelby's gaze softened as she cast a glance toward Felina before focusing on the screen.

"Before," Felina said. "Right before he shoved me off the back landing, he slid his hand in my pocket. I thought he was getting fresh. I was so shocked and then further stunned when he threw me off the landing. I had no idea he slid a nanodisc into my pocket until a little while ago."

"A nanodisc?" Shelby cocked an eyebrow. "What was on it?"

Felina lifted her chin toward the computer monitor. "Watch."

Moments later, Shelby emitted a low whistle. "I can't believe someone caught Crabtree's murder on video."

"Not someone," Remy said. "Our dead man, Willard Gaither."

Shelby's gaze met Remy's. "They stripped him naked looking for it and killed him when they didn't find it." She turned to Felina. "They must've figured he gave it to you, and they came looking for it in your apartment last night."

Felina nodded, a chill slipping down her spine.

Shelby reached out and touched Felina's arm. "I'm glad they didn't find you."

Felina read between the lines of Shelby's words. Her friend was glad whoever killed Gaither hadn't found Felina and turned her inside out, looking for the disk he'd slipped her.

"I guess you know I have to take that disk into evidence."

Landry popped the disk out of the computer and the sleeve and handed it over to Shelby.

Her lips quirked. "That was quick. You've already made a copy, haven't you?"

Remy laid a hand on Landry's shoulder. "Don't answer that." He smiled at his woman. "You'll let us know if the state police discover the identity of the two women?"

"It'll be on a need-to-know basis," Shelby said.

"We need to know," Lucas insisted. "If they're still

looking for this disk, they might come after Felina again."

Shelby gave him a tight smile. "I'll do my best to stay on top of it and pass on anything they find. I'm glad you have Felina's back. Take care of my friend," she said. "Friends are hard to come by, especially the good ones." She turned back to Remy. "So, what's your plan? I know it doesn't involve waiting for the state crime lab to get right on a six-month-old murder."

"Our plan is only available to those with a need-to-know," Lucas said with a grin.

Shelby chuckled. "Well, damn. You're beating me at my own game. But seriously…"

Remy cupped her cheek for a long moment, then dropped his hand and turned toward Swede, all teasing aside. "Swede, we could use your extraordinary data mining skills."

Swede dipped his head. "What are we looking for?"

"What Thomas spent his money on, and where," Remy said.

"Or who?" Shelby added.

"If it's possible," Lucas looked at the last frame frozen on the monitor. It was a sea of faces at Mardi Gras. "Could you tap into Gaither's client files? We'd like to know who hired him to follow Mr. Crabtree."

Swede nodded. "I'll give it my best shot."

"I bet Crabtree's wife hired Gaither to follow her

husband," Shelby said. "Especially if she suspected he was having an affair."

"Then why did Gaither wait until now to bring this video to Bayou Mambaloa?" Felina asked.

Lucas nodded. "And why was he at the Crawdad Hole, and not the Crabtree mansion?"

Remy grimaced. "Right now, we have more questions than answers. I'd like that to change soon."

"We all would," Hank said. "In the meantime, stay safe."

Lucas glanced at his watch. "It's getting close to four. I promised to get you back to the shop before four-thirty."

For the first time since she assumed ownership of the flower shop, she really had no desire to go there. She wanted to follow the threads and solve the mysteries of the two murders. She wouldn't feel safe, and the people of the town she loved so much could be in danger until the ones responsible were caught.

However, in the midst of uncertainty, life moved on.

She had customers counting on her to provide flowers for special occasions to express love, appreciation, pride in accomplishments and condolences for loss. She needed to be there for her community.

Lucas held out his hand. "Ready?"

She nodded, slipped her hand in his and smiled. "Thank you for being here for me."

"My pleasure." He lifted her hand and brushed a

soft kiss to the backs of her knuckles. "Really. I'm just glad I finally got your attention. I was running out of space in my room at the boarding house."

Felina looked at him closely. "Did you keep all those bouquets for yourself? There wasn't a girlfriend?"

He shook his head. "Only you. Every time I came in to order, you had an assistant help me at the counter."

"Oh, that would've been Anna. I don't use her often. She's a student in New Orleans and only comes to town between quarters. She's not full-time. But she can handle the front and take orders like a pro."

Lucas led her out of the war room and down the long hallway to the exit. "I was beginning to think you were avoiding me."

Felina's lips twisted. "I was probably too busy in the back to know you were even there." She squeezed his hand. "My loss and one of the reasons Marty mentioned for why our relationship was doomed."

"The man was a fool to let you go."

She shrugged. "I prefer to think of it as a timely parting. We weren't meant to be together. He made the leap where I would've just continued as we were. It was easier to do nothing than something."

"Then I'm glad he left you. He didn't deserve you. You need someone who is loyal and loving no matter

ELLE JAMES

how hard you work. Someone who is there when you get home and loves you no matter what."

Felina laughed. "You just described a golden retriever. Are you suggesting I get a dog rather than another man in my life?"

He grinned. "Why not both? There are men out there who appreciate a woman who's driven and ambitious." He leaned close, touching a finger beneath her chin, his mouth a breath away from hers. "Especially when she's passionate."

Felina forgot how to breathe.

Lucas was so close all she had to do was lean up a little, and their mouths would meet. Before she could make that move, he continued.

"Passionate about flowers." Lucas raised his head, grinning. "After your customers collect their items, do you want to get something to eat at the diner?"

She forced a laugh past the air lodged in her lungs. "A fake date with real food? I'm in."

Her breathing had barely returned to normal by the time they'd completed the short drive between the boat factory and her shop.

Lucas helped her down from the truck and walked with her to the front door.

After Felina unlocked the door, she flipped the sign to read OPEN and got to work, pushing the almost-kiss to the back of her mind. Why torture herself for not rising to make that connection when she had the chance?

Not long after she'd reopened the shop, the four orders were picked up.

Felina's belly rumbled. She went in search of Lucas and found him in her apartment, sweeping up broken glass. Drawers had been tucked back into her dresser, and the hanging clothes were lined up neatly in the closet. He'd even made the bed.

She smiled at the order he'd restored. "How did you do all this in such a short amount of time?"

"I learned how to be efficient and effective in bootcamp." He glanced around at his handiwork. "They didn't give us much time to screw up. If one person failed, the entire squad did pushups. You didn't want to be that one person."

Her lips twitched. "Your drill sergeant would be proud."

He gave a slight bow of his head. "Thank you."

"I locked the front door," she said.

"Will you be working on your orders now?" he asked as he tipped the dustpan into the trashcan.

Felina shook her head. "I lost my momentum. I don't have the energy or the heart to work tonight."

"I thought you had to get those orders in tonight, or they'd be late."

"I have a little wiggle room. I also thought I'd shut down the shop tomorrow after I get the deliveries out the door."

He raised his eyebrows. "You're going to close the shop?"

Felina nodded. "I thought we might drive into New Orleans. I can visit my distributor and place my order in person. Afterward, we could grab lunch. I know a really great restaurant that serves the most amazing crawfish etouffee."

"I'm always up for Cajun cuisine and playing hooky." His brow dipped low. "As long as you're comfortable with taking that time off."

"I am." Felina laughed. "I don't think I've had a day off during the week in the past five years."

"Then, you're long overdue. Taking the day off sounds like a plan." Lucas grinned. "For tomorrow. For now, we need to find something for dinner."

Her belly rumbled again. "Even as hungry as I am, I'd like to shower first."

"Need someone to scrub your back?" he asked.

Her heart fluttered, and butterflies beat at the lining of her stomach. He was teasing, right? Her eyes narrowed. "Is back scrubbing in your job description?"

"Yes, it is," he said. "It's in the fine print in the paragraph detailing the responsibilities of a fake boyfriend."

She laughed, amazed at how easy it was to talk to Lucas about something as intimate as him scrubbing her back. She'd have to be naked. And he'd have to be in the shower with her.

That sexy thought had her breath catching in her throat, making it hard for her to breathe normally.

Lucas might have been teasing about scrubbing her back, but Felina was serious about taking him up on it.

What about her vow to keep their relationship platonic? He was, after all, her employee. She was paying him to protect her, not make love to her.

Still, Lucas had offered...

And he'd made no move to leave her apartment.

Did she dare?

CHAPTER 10

TRYING to look and feel confident and sexy when she was nervous and needy, Felina strode into the small bathroom, reached around the shower curtain and turned on the water, fully aware of the open bathroom door.

She resisted looking over her shoulder. If he were interested, he'd be watching her every move.

Before she could chicken out, she reached for the button on her jeans, flicked it through the hole and slid the zipper down.

Cool air brushed against her belly, doing nothing to douse the fire burning at her core.

Slowly, she hooked her thumbs in the waistband of her jeans and eased them over her hips. Once the denim passed the curve of her ass, she slid one leg out and then the other.

She retrieved the condom from the back pocket

and then kicked the jeans to the side. She leaned into the shower and tucked the condom between her shampoo and conditioner as a reminder that sexy didn't have to be stupid.

Standing with her back to Lucas, Felina fought the urge to turn around and see if he was looking. Instead, she reached for the hem of her T-shirt and drew it up her torso.

Though she'd lamented the lack of a bra all day, now she was glad she wasn't wearing one. When she dropped the shirt on the floor, all that stood between her and naked was a thin scrap of lacy panties. She paused for a moment, hoping Lucas would take the hint and help her out of those panties.

When he didn't, she drew in a deep breath and slid the panties over her thighs and down past her calves, stepping free, proud of her striptease.

Now, she could look over her shoulder and give him that come-hither look she'd seen actresses do in movies.

Felina schooled her face, hoping she looked sexy, not stupid, and looked over her naked shoulder and straight into...

An empty room?

"Really?" she said out loud. "Here I am, baring my body and soul, and he chooses this moment to be a gentleman and give me privacy?"

Felina yanked back the shower curtain and climbed in, muttering, "So much for a back scrub."

She stepped beneath the spray, lathered her hair and lifted her face to the water when the shower curtain rings squeaked across the rod.

Felina spun, blinking moisture and soap out of her eyes.

Lucas stood naked in front of her, squirting soap into his hands. "What were you saying? I didn't quite catch the words."

"N-nothing?" she breathed. "Where—I didn't— you weren't—"

Stunned by his oh-my-God incredibly delicious nakedness so close she could touch, Felina couldn't form a coherent thought, much less an intelligent sentence. She couldn't process it all.

Lucas's lips curved into a smile that threatened the stability of Felina's knees. "Turn around," he said.

Her brain managed to react automatically to the command.

Felina turned. The shower's warm spray doused her front, rivulets of water dripping off the pebbled tips of her breasts.

Lucas's large, warm hands touched her back, spreading bubbles over her skin, smoothing across her shoulders, arms and down the center of her back.

Felina's head dropped back, her breathing grew ragged, and her core ignited into a flame so hot it threatened to consume her.

His hands wreaked havoc with her nerve endings, shooting electrical sparks throughout her body like the little metal ball in an antique pinball machine.

He leaned closer, his chest brushing against her, his hard cock nudging her buttocks. "Back scrubbing is complete."

Felina moaned. "Oh, please. Don't stop there." She reached around, captured his hands in hers and guided them to her breasts.

He didn't need any more encouragement and took it from there.

Lucas pressed his lips to the curve of her neck, his hands cupping her breasts to massage their fullness.

When he pinched the nipples gently between his thumbs and forefingers, Felina arched her back, leaning into him, wanting to feel his naked skin all across her body.

After teasing her breasts until she couldn't remember how to breathe, his hands moved lower, skimming across her ribs.

She sucked in air as those fingers moved even lower until they reached the apex of her thighs.

Lucas cupped her sex and pulled her closer. His cock pressed against her buttocks, hard and thick.

Felina's body ached with the need to feel him inside her. When he slid a finger between her folds and flicked her clit, she gasped and almost came at that point.

But he wasn't done with her.

He swirled around that nerve-packed nubbin,

flicked, touched and swirled again until Felina tensed, the force of her release teetering on the edge.

One more flick, and she didn't fall off the edge—she launched into orbit on wave after wave of energy ripping through her body.

Lucas played her sweet spot all the way to the end.

Her release only made her want more. She dragged in several shaky breaths before turning in Lucas's arms. "Tell me that was just a warmup," she whispered, pressing a kiss to his collarbone and another to his neck.

He chuckled. "That was just a warmup."

"Good." She slid her arm around his neck and brought his mouth down to hers. "Because I want more."

"Greedy little minx, are you?"

"Only because you make me that way."

He bent and scooped her up by her thighs while pressing her back against the tile wall. "As much as I want to fuck you against the wall, we need protection."

She laughed. "Gotcha covered." Felina reached for the condom between the shampoo and conditioner and held it up. "It was a gift from Gisele. She obviously saw the potential."

"Remind me to kiss that woman."

Felina frowned. "I'm already forgetting."

"Mmm. Scratch that." He brushed a kiss across

her nose. "Remind me to thank her. I'll save the kisses for my fake girlfriend."

"That's more like it." Felina wove her fingers into his damp hair and pulled him in for a kiss, her tongue slipping between his teeth to caress his.

The tip of his cock pressed against her entrance, thick, hard and insistent.

Felina broke the kiss and held up the condom. "Ready?"

He growled low in his throat. "More than ready."

After Felina tore open the packet and extracted the condom, Lucas lifted her enough she could roll it down over his engorged shaft. She fondled his balls for a few seconds and then braced her hands on his shoulders and locked her ankles around his waist.

Lucas lowered her, entering her slowly.

Her channel contracted around him, inviting him deeper until he was fully seated inside her.

His thick shaft filled her, making her feel complete like the missing piece had found its place.

Like coming home.

Then he moved.

The moist friction set off all new synapses, igniting nerve endings that stimulated her pleasure center into a tingling, excited state.

He pumped.

She rode him like the stallion he was, laughing out loud at the image conjured.

He slowed for just a second. "Something funny?"

"Not funny," she gasped. "Beautiful. For the love of Mike, don't stop!"

He renewed his efforts until his eyes closed and his body stiffened. One last thrust sent him so deep they were as one.

His cock pulsed his release.

The condom protected them both from any unwanted pregnancies.

For the first time in her life, Felina wished she hadn't used the condom. She'd always wanted children but had never felt the time was right.

So, why was she thinking it was right now?

Just because she'd had the best sex ever didn't mean the time was right to start a family.

Once Lucas's mission was over, he'd move on. He wouldn't have to pretend to be her boyfriend. As handsome as he was and as good as he was at sex, he'd have no problem finding a real girlfriend of his choice. Not one who'd paid him to pretend. For all she knew, this amazing lovemaking was nothing more than a one-night stand.

Lucas drew a deep breath, opened his eyes and smiled at her. "That was amazing." He leaned in to plant a kiss on her lips, a smile spreading across his face. "As great as it was, can you imagine how much better it will be in a bed?"

She gave him a weak smile. Was he suggesting they move to the bed? Did that mean this wasn't to be a one-night stand?

Felina didn't want to get her hopes up.

Then again, he'd bought more than half a dozen flower arrangements from her. His friend had said he'd only done it to get her attention.

He lifted her off his shaft, set her on the floor and kissed her again. The water was turning cooler, making Felina shiver.

"Let's rinse off and get out of here before all the hot water is gone."

Felina didn't want to miss the chance of running her fingers over his magnificent body. She squirted soap into her hands and quickly ran her fingers over his chest, shoulders and massive arms, then slid downward to his waist, hips and lower. She stripped the condom off and dropped it into the trash outside the shower, returning to grasp his still-hard cock.

She wanted to spend more time exploring her effect on him, but the water chose that moment to turn frigid.

"Holy ice cycles," she gasped.

Felina ducked beneath the spray, quickly rinsing off any remaining bubbles, then stepped out of the shower.

Lucas stayed a little longer. By the time he emerged, his cock wasn't nearly as stiff, and his skin was pebbled with goosebumps.

Felina handed him a towel.

Instead of drying himself off, he worked on her.

She returned the favor, getting more hands-on time with his muscles.

By the time they'd dried every inch of each other's bodies, Felina was ready to take it to the mattress.

Lucas swept her off her feet and carried her to the bed.

She smiled, looping her arm over his shoulder. "You read my mind."

"I read your body." He laid her across the comforter and nuzzled her neck. "Are you sure you want to do this more than getting a bite to eat?"

She hooked her hand around the back of his neck. "Why wait until the end of the meal to have dessert," she said in the sexiest voice she could manage.

Lucas laughed out loud.

Felina frowned. "That was supposed to be seductive."

"It was," he said, lying on the mattress beside her. "It's just that it was coming from you. Sweet, sassy Felina Faivre, Bayou Mambaloa's favorite flower girl."

She pouted. "How can we make love when you're laughing at me?"

"Oh, babe." Lucas chuckled. "Like this." Then he lowered his mouth to hers and kissed her senseless.

When he finally lifted his head, he was still grinning. "Convinced?"

"Mmm. I might need a little more of that before I buy it."

"Then let me give you the full sales job." He kissed her thoroughly, dueling with her tongue for a long moment before abandoning her mouth to move lower. "Mmm. Much better to have my hands free to do this." While kissing a path down the length of her neck, his fingers blazed their own path to her breasts.

He pinched the tip of her nipple between his thumb and forefinger, rolling it until it formed a tight little bead. Then, his mouth caught up, and he traded fingers for tongue, flicking the nipple until Felina's back arched off the bed.

He treated her other breast to the same delicious sensations while his hand skimmed across her ribs and downward to cup her sex.

Felina raised her hips.

Lucas dipped a finger into her wet channel and swirled around. With his digit soaked in her juices, he slid between her folds and teased her clit until she writhed beneath him.

His lips left her breast and skimmed across her torso, ever downward, until he nestled between her thighs and touched his tongue to that one place that sent her into a spinning, whirling place of ultimate ecstasy.

Felina dug her fingers into his hair as he played her, flicking, licking and swirling until she came apart in a million points of light.

She held onto that sensation for as long as she could, then collapsed onto the mattress, breathing hard, her heart racing and laughter bubbling up inside.

Lucas rose over her, his cock nudging her entrance. "Now, who's laughing?"

"I don't know why," she said, settling into light chuckles. "I guess it just felt so good."

"It did."

She wrapped her legs around him, her heels digging into his buttocks. "Are you up for round two?"

Lucas closed his eyes, his jaw hardening. "I want it, but I'm not ready." He opened his eyes and tipped his head toward the pile of clothes on one of the kitchenette chairs. "I have only one condom in my wallet. We can use it now or have dinner and a second dessert later."

"Or, we can have our second dessert now and run by the store when we're out for dinner." She smiled up at him. "Can your sweet tooth handle a third dessert?"

"I can't get enough sweets," he said and pressed a kiss to her lips. "Hold that thought."

He leaped out of the bed, strode across the room, fished the condom out of his wallet and was back in under five seconds.

They made love again, using the last condom. Felina wasn't worried. They were going to buy more. The one-night stand wouldn't be for only one night.

She decided not to look too far ahead. If their

time together was only until after Trish and Marty's wedding, then at least they'd have fun while it lasted. She'd have the rest of her life to get over Lucas.

And it might take all the rest of her life to forget him.

She'd never felt this strongly about Marty. Not even when they'd started dating back in high school. It had just been the thing to do—having a boyfriend.

Now that she knew what love should feel like, she'd never settle for anything less.

Which might mean she'd be single for the rest of her life. Seriously. How many men could there be out there that could melt her panties with a single glance?

An hour later, Lucas held the door for Felina and followed her down the stairs outside her apartment. "Where to?"

"The diner has the best meatloaf in the parish," she said.

"Meatloaf?" he asked, frowning.

Felina cocked an eyebrow. "You've been in Bayou Mambaloa for how long?"

The florist's sassy expression made Lucas want to kiss her all over again. But that would make him want to throw her over his shoulder, march back up to her apartment and make love to her for the third time that afternoon.

His stomach rumbled. "I haven't had the pleasure of Bayou Mambaloa's famous meatloaf. I will remedy that lack of culinary experience ASAP."

Felina looked down her nose with her snootiest glance. "As you should."

"It's a beautiful evening." He held out his hand. "Shall we walk?"

"I'd love that." Felina placed her hand in his.

As they strolled along the sidewalk to the diner a couple of blocks away, Lucas couldn't remember the last time he'd been so at peace with himself and the person he was with.

Felina was the reason. All the weeks of buying flower arrangements he hadn't needed hadn't been in vain. He'd known Felina was special by the way she was with others and the way other people treated her. Her community loved her and the joy she delivered with each bouquet.

Making love with her had been just as wonderful. He didn't want any of it to end.

They arrived at Tante Mimi's Diner near the tail-end of the dinner rush.

Lucas had been here a number of times with some of the guys staying at the boarding house.

The black-haired, green-eyed female owner of the diner sailed by with a tray full of food balanced on her shoulder. "Find a table you like. I'll be by to clean it in just a minute."

"Thanks, Mimi," Lucas responded.

Felina shot him a narrow-eyed glance.

He held up his hands. "What?"

"I thought you said you hadn't had the meatloaf at the diner."

"I haven't. I always get the chicken-fried steak." He grinned. "Those of us staying at the boarding house eat here a lot."

Felina shook her head. "And you haven't had the meatloaf."

He laid a hand over his heart. "It's a character flaw I hope to overcome."

Felina's lips twitched, and a smile broke through. "You're in for a treat."

"Another?" He rested a hand against the small of her back. "Can't wait for the third dessert."

Felina's cheeks turned a pretty shade of pink as she slid into a booth.

Lucas sat across from her.

As promised, Mimi arrived with a tray, cleared the empty plates and cups and wiped the table with a clean rag. "What can I get you? The usual?" She nodded toward Felina. "Meatloaf?"

Felina nodded.

Mimi smiled at Lucas. "Chicken-fried steak?"

Lucas met Felina's gaze. "Not today. I've been told your meatloaf is the best. I'm willing to give it a try."

"Two meatloaf plates coming up." Mimi hefted the platter onto her shoulder and disappeared through the swinging door into the kitchen.

The door to the diner opened, and two older women entered, talking all the way to a table at the center of the room.

Mimi emerged from the kitchen. "Mrs. Dupuy, Mrs. Gentry, I'm surprised to see you." She hurried over to clear the table of the dirty dishes and wiped it clean. "I thought tonight was bridge night."

The ladies smiled, shaking their heads.

The woman in the pale peach pantsuit sat in a chair and placed her handbag on the seat beside her. "It's supposed to be, but Brenda and Missy claimed to be too busy getting ready for Colonial Day to bother with bridge."

The other woman wore a soft gray sleeveless dress. She took the seat across the table from her friend. "You'd think they had to do the actual physical preparation. They hire all the help, just like us."

"Do you know what you want off the menu?" Mimi asked.

"Could you give us a minute?"

"Sure," Mimi smiled. "While you're waiting, would you like coffee or tea?"

"Tea, please," both ladies answered at the same time.

Mimi left to fetch their drinks.

Lucas leaned over the table toward Felina. "Are you doing the flowers for these two ladies?"

Felina nodded, lifted a finger to her lips and whispered, "The one in peach is Lola Dupuy of Magnolia

Blossom Estate. The other is Martha Gentry of Harmony Grove Plantation. All are on the Colonial Day tour map. And, yes, I've got all their places. If anyone knows anything, it would be these ladies. Their sources are deeply entrenched in the community."

Lucas nodded his understanding of what Felina was saying without saying it. Now would be a good time to shut up and listen.

Mimi returned with a tray containing two teacups, a teapot full of hot water, a small creamer and a container filled with packets of sugar and sweetener alternatives. She laid the items on the table along with an assortment of tea bags. "Colonial Day is just around the corner. I love seeing the old places turned out like they were when they were originally built. I'm sure it takes some planning. Are you two ready?"

"As ready as we'll ever be."

"Could I get the club sandwich without bacon?" Martha said.

Mimi nodded. "Do you want potato chips or fries?"

"Neither." Martha smiled. "Just the sandwich."

"I'll have the French onion soup," Lola handed the menu to Mimi.

"Colonial Day is exhausting and gets a little more competitive each year," Martha Gentry said, continuing the conversation as if it hadn't been interrupted. "I'll never understand why there's such a big deal."

"Because we have the four finest historic homes in the parish, and the most beautiful one gets a full-page spread in the Southern Homes magazine." Lola shook her head. "Personally, I could care less about the magazine article. No one buys magazines anymore. It's all silly how many hoops we jump through each year just for one day. You don't know how many times I've wanted to sell the place, find an apartment in New York City and never again set foot inside the smelly, sweaty, bug and alligator-infested state of Louisiana."

"Now, you're sounding like Brenda," Martha said. "Which blows my mind. I thought for sure she'd sell as soon as Thomas passed."

Lola nodded. "I thought the same. Lord knows she's had enough investors knocking on her door. And it would serve the bastard right if she sold it. She stuck with him all these years when she should've divorced him a long time ago. She had to know he was cheating on her for practically her entire marriage."

Martha wrinkled her nose. "His business meetings in Baton Rouge were convenient." She lifted the teapot and poured steaming water into her cup and then Lola's. "My son, Ryan, the one who lives in Baton Rouge, swears he saw Thomas at Fleming's one night, several years ago. And he wasn't alone. He had a woman with him who wasn't Brenda. The maître d' seated them in one of the secluded tables at the back of the restaurant."

Lola dropped a teabag into her cup of hot water. "There was a time, perhaps a decade ago, he made a pass at me." She patted her short, silvery hair. "He'd had a little too much whiskey at the country club. I shut him down immediately. Brenda herded him out and drove him home."

"I wouldn't blame her if she was the one who killed him," Martha said.

"Me either." Lola dipped a teabag into her cup and then set it to the side on the saucer. "But I can't see her stabbing him. Too messy. Poison? Now, that would be more her style."

Martha nodded. "She won't even putter in her own gardens because she doesn't like to get her hands dirty or destroy her manicure. Still, she was lucky that her gardener could vouch for her whereabouts. The police always look to the people closest to the victim, and Brenda had plenty of motive."

"I can't believe it's been six months," Lola lifted her teacup, "and they still don't have a suspect."

Martha tore open a packet of sweetener and poured it into her cup. "You'd think that with all the people around him at that parade, someone would've seen it happen."

Someone had, Lucas thought. And had withheld evidence. Why?

Lola poured cream into her tea. "Now, Brenda has that big old house to deal with. It was Thomas's pride and joy. Not hers. She's probably waiting for the best offer."

Martha frowned. "Then why, for heaven's sake, did she enter it in the Colonial Day tour this year?"

"To spite Missy?" Lola suggested. "You know how much Missy wants that spread in the magazine. She's gotten it almost every year since God knows when. I thought about jazzing up Magnolia Blossom just once to get her goat." Lola's smile twisted. "Then I thought of all the money I'd waste just to prove what?" She shrugged. "Not much. I spent the money on a trip to the French Riviera. It was much more satisfying than playing games with the locals."

Martha chuckled. "I'm with you."

Mimi appeared beside Lucas and Felina's table, carrying a tray loaded with their meals. She laid the plates down in front of them and straightened. "Can I get you two anything else?"

"No, thank you," Felina said.

When Mimi headed back to the kitchen, Lucas glanced toward the table where the two ladies were sitting.

Both women were staring at him and Felina.

"Felina, darling," Lola called out. "I didn't see you there. How are you, my dear?"

Felina smiled, her cheeks flushing a soft pink. "Fine, thank you."

"I suppose you'll be providing the florals for Crabtree Manor after all?" Lola cocked a well-drawn eyebrow.

"Yes, ma'am," Felina said.

"You'll have your hands full. Do you have sufficient help to handle it all?" Lola asked.

Felina nodded. "I will. I have people on standby as usual to handle the deliveries."

"And I'm sure your new man will be there for the heavy lifting." Lola dipped her head in Lucas's direction.

The color in Felina's cheeks deepened. "Have you met my...boyfriend?" she asked.

"No, we have not, though we've seen a few new men in town around the boat factory."

"Ladies, this is Lucas LeBlanc."

Lucas stood and walked over to the women. He took Lola's hand and brushed his lips across her knuckles while staring into her eyes. "Pleasure to meet you."

He did the same for Martha. "Pleasure to meet you." Then he returned to the booth and slid onto the bench.

"What a gentleman," Lola said. "You better hold onto that one."

"And don't leave him alone with your friends," Martha added.

Felina's smile tightened but didn't slip. "I'll keep that in mind."

Lucas reached across the table and took her hand in his, squeezing gently.

She gave him a grateful smile. "You're gonna love the meatloaf."

He dug into the meal. As Felina had predicted, he loved the meatloaf.

On the other side of the table, Felina picked at her plate full of food.

When Lucas was finished, Felina asked Mimi to bring a box so that she could take her food back to her apartment.

Once outside the diner, Lucas asked, "What's wrong?"

Felina continued walking. "Who said anything's wrong?"

"You didn't eat the meatloaf you advertised as to-die-for."

"I just wasn't that hungry." She held up the box. "But I brought it with me for when I do get hungry again." She gave him a tight smile.

"Was it something I said?" he persisted.

Felina shook her head. "No."

"Did the ladies' comment about keeping this one strike a nerve?"

Felina lifted one shoulder and let it drop. "It doesn't matter. I don't know why I let comments like that bother me. For that matter, I don't know why I felt driven to hire a fake boyfriend. When you leave me, it'll only reinforce what they think." She sighed. "That I can't maintain a relationship."

"Your ex-boyfriend was the one who couldn't maintain a relationship," Lucas pointed out. "You didn't cheat on him."

"He wouldn't have felt the need to seek out love somewhere else if I'd shown him a little more affection."

"You said it yourself that you weren't in love with him." He stopped and turned her to face him. "Were you in love with Marty?"

She shook her head. "No. But then, what is love?" She stared up into his eyes. "Passion?"

He shook his head. "Passion is great and all, but it wanes. Love is something that endures."

"Why?"

"Because the people who fall in true love aren't just lovers. They're friends and like spending time together, even if it's working together. They respect each other and care about each other."

"What if only one person in the relationship has that kind of love?" she asked. "Is it doomed?"

Lucas didn't have the answer to that question. "Maybe. Although, the one who isn't in love could learn to love that person over time." He wasn't sure where the conversation was going, but his gut told him it was important to Felina.

"How much time?" she asked.

Lucas shrugged. "Think about arranged

marriages. Over time, many of the participants grow to love and respect each other."

"It doesn't matter. It's not like I'm going to fall in love any time soon or anyone is going to fall in love with me. I barely have time to date. Relationships take time. I didn't give my last one time to make it work."

Lucas tipped her chin up. "Had you really loved him, you would've found the time."

"That's just it. How do you know when it's love?" she asked.

He stared down into her eyes. "When you can't imagine life without that person in it. When you ache inside when you're apart. When you want that person to be the first face you see in the morning and the last one you see before you close your eyes at night. When the sound of her voice makes you feel like you've come home." He cupped her cheek and brushed his thumb across her lips.

"Have you ever felt that way?" she whispered.

He nodded. "Yes."

"She must have been special," Felina said.

"Yes." He bent and brushed his lips across hers. "When you know...you know."

He kissed her again, wanting to tell her he knew he loved her and had loved her from the first time he saw her standing in the doorway of her shop holding a bouquet of flowers for an elderly man. She'd followed him out to his truck and helped secure the vase in the front seat to get it home to his wife.

He wasn't sure she was ready to know he loved her. Her confidence had been shaken when Marty had walked out on her and proposed to her best friend. Lucas needed to take his time with her and let her come to see that he was the one for her.

For now, he'd have to be content with a kiss. And if he kissed her often enough, and she liked it, she'd eventually realize she could kiss him until death did they part.

She opened to his kiss, meeting his tongue with hers. Her empty hand reached up and encircled the back of his neck, urging him closer.

A cell phone chirped.

Lucas ignored it, lost in the magic of their kiss.

It chirped again.

Felina stiffened.

On the third chirp, she looked up into his eyes. "It's mine." She stepped back and dug into her purse with her free hand.

Lucas took the box of food from her.

On the fifth ring, Felina finally pulled her phone out and stared down at the screen. "It's Trish."

"Answer it," he said. The moment was already past.

Felina hit the receive button and held the phone to her ear. "Hey, Trish."

Her friend spoke fast.

Felina frowned. "Hey, slow down. What? Why? No. Don't do anything until we've had a chance to talk." She nodded. "No, I'm not doing anything. I'll be right there." She ended the call and looked up at Lucas. "I have to go. Trish is upset about something and wants to call off the wedding. I told her not to make any decisions until we had a chance to talk. I have to go." She grimaced. "Can I get a raincheck on the third dessert?"

Lucas smiled. "Always." He hooked her arm and steered her toward her shop. "Come on, I'll take you there in my truck."

"You don't have to. I can drive my car."

He shook his head. "I'm still your fake boyfriend until the wedding."

She frowned. "There might not be a wedding. Trish was pretty upset."

"I'm sure after you talk with her, all will be well, and the wedding will go off without a hitch," he said.

They arrived at the shop and went straight to his truck.

"What if it isn't Trish wanting to call it off?" Felina said. "What if Marty changed his mind?"

Lucas paused before he opened the door for her. "It's possible." He tipped his head. "He could've realized what a fool he was for walking away from you. As we speak, he might be on his way here to beg you to take him back."

Felina stared up at him, a frown denting her brow. "You think he'd do that?"

Lucas prayed he was wrong. "He could be coming to his senses. Now, if it had been me, I never would've left you." He pulled open the truck door. "We could stay here and see if he shows up."

Felina snorted. "Even if he did show up, begging me to come back to him, he'd be wasting his time. He did us both a favor by walking out on me." She climbed into the truck. "I don't love Marty. I don't think I ever did."

Lucas fought back a grin. "How do you know?"

She grinned. "When you know you're not in love...you know."

He closed the door and rounded the truck, a smile spreading across his face. At least she knew she didn't love her ex-boyfriend. Now, all she had to do was realize that she loved him.

That might take a bit. She had a huge number of orders to deliver for Colonial Day and a wedding to do. Until those were behind her, she wouldn't have time to think, much less listen to her heart.

Lucas would have to be patient and make himself indispensable. He could do that.

Felina was worth it.

CHAPTER 11

LUCAS PULLED up in front of the little cottage Trish rented on the edge of town, shifted into park and started to get out of the truck.

Felina laid a hand on his arm. "I'm sure Trish isn't going to want to spill her guts with you looking over my shoulder."

"I'm only going to walk you to the door. I won't go in with you," Lucas said. "I just want to make sure you're safe. Then I'll wait in the truck."

Felina shook her head before he finished speaking. "If you're hanging around, she might feel like I'd rather be somewhere else." Which was true. Felina would rather be back at her apartment partaking of dessert number three.

"Fine," he said. "I'll pretend to leave, drive around the block and park out of her sight. But I'm not leaving you anywhere. We still don't know who broke into your apartment. He might be watching you, waiting for me to leave you alone so he can swoop in."

"Okay, okay. I get the picture. I'm convinced. And yes, I don't want you too far away, especially considering there's a murderer out there somewhere. Gaither knew her and probably died because of that knowledge. I just need a little time alone with Trish. She was very upset."

Lucas's eyes narrowed. "Have you considered the fact that the murderer was female?"

Felina tipped her head. "We know the murderer was a female from the video."

He continued to stare at her.

"What? You think Trish could be the murderer?" Felina shook her head. "No way. Trish is a lover, not a killer. She couldn't even squash a bug. She catches spiders she finds in her house and releases them outside."

"And people thought the BTK killer was a fine, upstanding member of his church."

"Trish is not a murderer." Felina unbuckled her seatbelt and looped her purse over her shoulder.

Lucas reached under his seat and pulled out a wicked black knife in a sheath. "At least take this. If you feel threatened, you'll have some protection."

Her lips pressed together. "I'm not taking that knife."

"Take the knife, or I'll have to go in with you." His jaw tightened.

Felina opened the door and climbed out.

Lucas climbed out as well, meeting her at the front of the truck.

She marched to the front door and rang the bell.

Lucas remained with her, the knife in his hand.

The sound of footsteps made Felina's heart beat faster. As the footsteps reached the door, Felina grabbed the knife from Lucas and shoved it to the bottom of her purse. "There. Are you happy?"

"Only mildly," he said. "I'd feel better if I were going in with you."

"Well, you're not."

The door swung open.

Trish stood there in shorts and a baggy T-shirt, her hair in wild disarray, her cheeks damp, and her eyes red and puffy. "Oh, Felina," she cried.

"Hey, sweetie." As soon as Felina stepped into the house, Trish fell into her arms.

Still standing in the doorway, Felina held her friend for a long moment.

When Trish finally raised her head, she looked out at Lucas. "Do you...want to...come in?" she asked between hiccups.

Lucas opened his mouth.

Before he could say anything, Felina answered for him, "He has some errands to run that could take a long time. I'll call him when I'm ready to leave.

How about I make us some iced tea, and we can talk?"

"I don't know what good it will do. My life is ruined."

Felina faced Lucas and mouthed, *I'll be okay*, then closed and locked the door. She followed Trish to the little kitchen. "Talk to me, Trish. What's so bad we can't fix it with tea and a hug?"

The brunette stopped in the middle of the kitchen and looked around as if lost. "I did something..." she hiccupped, and more tears slid down her face, "stupid. I thought...I could...handle it...now..." She faced Felina, her face crumpling. "I can't. I have to...call off...the wedding."

Felina took her friend's hand and led her to the table. "Sit. I'll make the tea."

"There's no...other...way." Trish buried her face in her hands.

"There's always another way," Felina said as she filled the electric kettle with water. "We just have to put our heads together and find it." After she turned on the kettle, she sat at the table with Trish and took her hands. "First, you have to tell me what's wrong. I can't help you fix it if I don't know what it is."

"I can't tell you," she said. "You already hate me."

"I don't hate you," Felina insisted. "Just tell me what's wrong. Is it Marty?"

"Yes...no..." She burst into a fresh round of sobs. "He'll hate me, too."

"Trish, nothing you could do would make us hate you."

"Yes, you will." She stared at their hands, refusing to look Felina in the eyes.

"You're sweet, kind and loveable."

Finally, she looked up. "How can you say that when I stole your boyfriend?"

"You didn't steal him. We didn't love each other. We would've broken up anyway."

"But I never should've started seeing him while you were still together."

The water came to a boil, and the kettle shut off automatically with a loud click.

Trish released Felina's hands and pushed to her feet.

"The tea can wait," Felina said.

"No. It's okay," Trish turned and walked into the living room. "I have to keep packing."

Felina left the tea and the kitchen. "Packing? Why?"

"I'm leaving tomorrow."

"Are you moving in with Marty?" Felina asked.

Trish shook her head. "No. I can't marry Marty. I can't stay here. I have to leave." She went into the bedroom and came out carrying a box overflowing with stuff jammed into it. "Will you donate this stuff to the women's shelter or Goodwill? I can't take it with me. I only have so much room in my car."

"Sweetie, give it to me." Felina held out her arms.

Trish handed her the box and returned to her bedroom for another.

Felina set the box beside others on the floor containing books, clothes, figurines, shoes...everything Trish had collected over the years.

"Why do you have to leave?" Felina followed her friend into the bedroom. "What could be so bad that you'd leave your home, friends and family?"

Trish held a box in her arms. "I have to leave. I'm out of money. I'm going to lose my business, and they'll only want more."

Felina frowned. "Who wants more?"

Still holding the box, Trish sank onto the bed. "I thought it was over. I never wanted him to die, but when it happened, I thought it was over." She shook her head. "It's not. If I don't pay them, they'll go to Marty. I can't sell the house. It isn't mine. Neither is my beauty shop. I rent it. I'm done. I have nothing left to give."

Felina sat down beside her friend. "Talk to me, Trish. Who are you paying?" She stared at her friend. "Is someone blackmailing you?"

Trish's eyes filled with tears. "They said if I told anyone, they'd kill me, my friends and my family. They'd kill Marty. And they will." She looked into Felina's eyes. "They killed the first guy who was making me pay—the guy they found in the bayou. I was supposed to meet him that night at the Crawdad Hole. He said he had something for me. When I got there, he was already gone. Then he turned up in the bayou."

"You were meeting Gaither that night?" Felina's gut knotted.

"He said he was done." She stared into the box. "I wouldn't have to pay anymore if I met him that night."

"What was he using to blackmail you?"

"I can't." She turned away from Felina. "You should go. You don't want to get mixed up with me. The only way I can be free, and my family, friends and Marty will be safe, is for me to either leave or die."

"Neither choice is an option." Felina took the box from her friend. As she moved to set it aside, something bright royal blue caught her attention. She pulled out a white blouse and a pair of denim shorts and gaped at what lay beneath them.

Her hand shook as she lifted a mask made of bright blue feathers and rhinestones. Under the mask was a sequined dress in matching royal blue.

"Go, Felina." Trish turned to face Felina. "If you like that, take it. I never want to see it again. Or any of this stuff. Tell Marty I'm sorry for breaking you two up. I didn't mean to fall in love with him. It's just that when you know, you know. I couldn't help myself." She broke down sobbing again.

"Trish," Felina said, her heart lodged in her throat. "Stop. Crying."

"I c-can't." She cried even more.

"Trish!" Felina's tone must have gotten through to her.

She lifted her head, scrubbing the tears from her eyes. "What?"

"Where were you the day Thomas Crabtree was murdered?"

Trish's eyes rounded. She sat perfectly still. She lifted her chin, a resigned look on her face. "I was in New Orleans."

"With Thomas Crabtree?" Felina couldn't believe what her friend was saying. This wasn't happening. Trish was kind, sweet and gentle.

Trish nodded. "I was. But it's not what you think."

"What should I think?" Felina asked.

"I wasn't having an affair with him if that's what you're thinking." She drew in a breath and let it out. "He hired me to go places with him—restaurants, art galleries and other old plantation houses like his. He was interested in history and didn't like going alone. My hair business wasn't making enough money to pay the rent on the shop and the house. Until things picked up, I had to take part-time work."

"As a prostitute?" Felina looked at Trish. Did she really know this woman?

"No, of course not." Trish stood and paced the length of the small room and back. "As an escort. It all started when I was cutting Thomas's hair one day. I told him I had to get another job to make ends meet. He offered to help. All I had to do was go places with him, and he'd pay me a lot more than if I got a job at a burger joint."

"If something sounds too good to be true, it probably is," Felina said. "What else did you have to do for the money?"

Trish held up her hands. "I told him flat out I wouldn't have sex with him, and if he ever tried anything, the deal was off. He agreed. I went with him on several 'dates.' The money was good. I was able to pay off my credit cards, pay my rent and put some money aside."

"Didn't you feel at all bad for Mrs. Crabtree?"

"I wasn't trying to take her husband away, nor was I having an affair with him. I was just a companion who listened to him talk about history."

Felina could see where Thomas was coming from. His wife could have cared less about history, old plantation houses or listening to her husband talk about them.

"Then Marty and I bumped into each other at the coffee shop. We shared the only empty table and talked. As friends. When we looked up, three hours had passed. After that, we bumped into each other at the coffee shop every day. We didn't go looking for love. It found us." She shook her head. "I don't expect you to understand. He left you for me. That was enough betrayal on both our parts. But when you find the one...you can't imagine spending a single day without him. You don't want to spend any more time apart than you have to. And you want his face to be the last one you see at night and the one you wake to in the morning."

Almost verbatim, those were the words Lucas had said to her that day.

All the time she'd been in Trish's cottage, she imagined Lucas driving around the block and parking where he could watch the house. Knowing he was out there helped. She still wanted him beside her. Especially now.

"The day Thomas was killed, I'd gone with him to the Mardi Gras parade as planned. I waited until we were there to tell him it would be our last outing together. Business was picking up, and I had found someone I wanted to spend all my free time with. He said he understood and wished me happiness. I kissed his cheek and left, eager to get back to Bayou Mambaloa and the coffee shop."

Trish stopped pacing and stared at Felina. "You don't know how many times I wished I'd stayed just a little longer. I should've been with him and walked him back to his car or hotel. If I had, he might not be dead. I feel responsible for Thomas Crabtree's death."

"Did you kill him?" Felina asked.

Trish's eyes widened. "Of course not."

"Then don't beat yourself up for it." Felina's eyebrows drew together. "You say someone was blackmailing you."

She nodded. "Shortly after Thomas's death, a man showed up at my house with an envelope full of pictures of me and Thomas together. By then, I was in love with Marty and didn't want anything to come between us.

"This man never told me his name, just showed me the pictures. I knew no one would believe me if I told them I wasn't having an affair with Thomas. I never slept with him. The only time I kissed him was when I said goodbye—and that was on his cheek.

"He told me he wanted a thousand dollars for the pictures.

"I told him to go to hell. I didn't want them to get out and ruin my chances with Marty, but I also resented being at the mercy of this man."

Trish looked away. "Then he told me that because I was with Thomas at the same time he was murdered, I'd be a prime suspect. All they had to do was send the pictures to the New Orleans Police Department, and they'd come looking for me. I'd be arrested and thrown in jail. Since I couldn't afford bail, I'd be there until the trial. They'd plant the knife used in the murder in my house. I'd be convicted and spend the rest of my life being someone's bitch."

"So, you paid the thousand dollars."

"I was scared. Who was going to believe me? The pictures were damning." Trish snorted. "He gave them to me. I immediately burned them. I thought it was over and got on with my life. Marty proposed, he left you and we planned our wedding. Everything was great until I got the text to meet him at the Crawdad Hole. He had something for me."

"I was there, but I missed him. Then he turned up dead. It was a relief for me. He wouldn't harass me to make payments. I was happy and ready to throw myself into wedding preparations until last night. Two men showed up at my house, demanding I pay to keep images of me and Thomas Crabtree from getting into the hands of the detectives working the case. They wanted ten thousand dollars. I told them I didn't have that much money. I'd have to sell everything, and I'd still be short."

"Is that when you decided leaving would be your only option?"

"No." She lifted her chin and met Felina's gaze. "It was when they promised to hurt everyone I cared about, starting with Marty. And that is why I have to leave. Before morning."

Felina stood. "You're not going anywhere but straight to the police department."

Trish's eyes widened. "No. I can't. They said that if I go to the police, they'll target Marty. They know where he lives. I can't do that to him. This was my mess. I have to leave to keep him safe. They're watching me."

Felina frowned. "At the very least, we have to let Shelby know. They're already looking for the people who nabbed Gaither. They could be the ones who are now blackmailing you."

"I can't go to the police," Trish said.

Felina thought for a moment. If they were watching Trish's place, they'd know who was coming or going. If Trish left, they'd follow her straight to the sheriff's office. Unless...

Felina went to Trish's closet, pulled out jeans and a nice blouse, and handed them to Trish. "Here. Change into these."

"I told you, I can't go to the sheriff or any other law enforcement agency."

"Just do it," Felina commanded. "And fix your hair and makeup."

"You don't understand."

"I get it. We're not going to the sheriff's office. We're going to the Crawdad Hole for a girls' night out with friends."

"I don't feel like going out. I have to leave by morning."

Felina gripped Trish's arms and leaned close. "If we can't go to the police or sheriff's department, they can come to us. We're going for a girls' night out with friends. If one of our friends happens to be a sheriff's deputy, no big deal."

Trish's eyes widened. "They'll be watching me."

"Then all they'll see is you hanging out with your girlfriends."

"Marty doesn't know about any of this. If they suspect I've gone to the law, they'll hurt Marty."

"Lucas has friends. They can protect you and Marty until we figure this thing out."

Trish stepped out of her shorts and pulled on the jeans. "Do you think it'll work?" She pulled the over-sized T-shirt over her head, then dragged the blouse up over her arms and buttoned the front. "I'm scared."

"Yeah. Well, so am I." When she pulled her cell phone from her purse, her fingers brushed against the knife Lucas had insisted on her carrying. It didn't give her the slightest bit of assurance that she could use it to protect herself. Maybe from the woman who'd killed Thomas. But she doubted it would be enough to go up against the guys who'd killed Gaither.

CHAPTER 12

WHEN LUCAS GOT the call from Felina to come pick her up, he hadn't expected Trish to climb into the back seat of the truck.

Felina grinned as she stepped up on the running board. "We decided tonight would be a good night to go to the Crawdad Hole for a girls' night out. Do you mind taking us?" She was speaking louder than usual, and the smile on her face appeared strained.

Lucas wasn't sure what was going on, but he went along with it. "I don't mind at all."

Felina slid onto the passenger seat and closed the door.

As soon as they left Trish's Street, Felina dialed a number on her cell phone. "Hey, Shelby. Can you meet me and Trish at the Crawdad Hole for girls' night out?" She listened for a moment. "I know we had one this week already, but, trust me, we need another. You do? Good. We'll see you there. Oh, and leave the uniform and service vehicle at home." Felina ended the call and glanced over her shoulder at Trish. "Shelby's on her way."

Lucas glanced in the rearview mirror. Trish had washed the tears from her face and applied a little makeup, but her eyes were still red-rimmed, and her face appeared strained.

"What's going on?" he asked.

"We found blue girl," Felina said softly.

"Oh, yeah?" Lucas shot a glance toward Felina. "Who is she?"

Felina tipped her head toward Trish.

Lucas's gaze shot to the rearview mirror and the reflection of a young, very distraught woman. He shifted his gaze to Felina. "Shouldn't we be going somewhere besides a bar?"

Felina glanced out the window, checked the side mirror and turned in her seat to look out the back window of the truck before turning her attention to Lucas. "We're doing what we can. We're gonna need one of your guys to go to Marty's place with some pizza or burgers and hang out until further notice."

Trish leaned through the seat, her face animated for the first time since climbing into the truck. "Please. He could use a friend about now."

"A friend with skills," Felina added.

Lucas's foot left the accelerator. "Do you mind telling me what's going on?"

She glanced in the side mirror and out the back window again. "The short version is Trish is being blackmailed, first by Gaither and then by another man who sounds a lot like the one I saw push Gaither into the SUV. They have photos, most likely those we found on the disk, of her with Thomas Crabtree, which would imply she was having an affair with the man."

"I wasn't. I never slept with him." Trish laid a hand on Felina's shoulder. "I was just a companion to him for a couple of months. We went to museums and historical plantation houses. Nothing else. The Mardi Gras parade was going to be my last paid outing with him." She sat back in her seat. "It was his last outing with me and anyone else."

Felina patted her friend's hand. "If Trish doesn't come up with ten thousand dollars by tomorrow, they've threatened to hurt Marty and anyone she cares about."

"They said that if I go to the police, they'll kill Marty and send the photos to the police. Because I was with Thomas the day he was killed, I'll be charged with his murder."

Lucas's foot returned to the accelerator, the reason for the call to Shelby and the girls' night out becoming clear. "So, if you can't go to the sheriff..."

"She'll come to us." Felina leaned back in her seat and stared at the road ahead. "Trish was the blue girl. She didn't kill Thomas Crabtree."

"I was there at the parade, but I left before..." Trish bit her lip. "I left when I should've stayed. Then none of this would have happened."

"It's not your fault," Felina assured her. And to Lucas, she said, "Shelby has some information for us as well. She didn't say what but will tell us when we're together."

Lucas pulled his cell phone out of his pocket and called Remy.

"Hey, Lucas," Remy answered. "Everything all right?"

Lucas turned onto Main Street and headed for the Crawdad Hole just past the marina. "We have blue girl."

"What do you mean?" Remy asked. "From the video?"

"That's the one. Meet me at the Crawdad Hole as soon as possible. Bring one of the guys with you. And send one of our guys with pizza and beer to Marty's place. Felina will give you the address. Make sure he's armed and prepared to stay for a while. Same for whoever you bring with you. I have a mission for him. I'll fill you in when we meet at the bar."

"On it," Remy said. "I'll be there in ten minutes."

Lucas handed his cell phone to Felina. "Give him Marty's address."

While Felina gave Remy the address, Lucas pulled into the parking lot of the Crawdad Hole and shifted into park. He'd been watching in the rearview mirror, looking for any indication that they were being followed, but had yet to detect any vehicles tailing them.

He climbed down from the truck and helped Trish and Felina to the ground. Then, with an arm around each woman, he escorted them to the door with a smile pasted on his face. "You two enjoy. I'll be your designated driver when you're ready to leave."

Felina leaned up and brushed her lips across his. "Thanks, babe." Then she hooked her arm through Trish's, pinned a smile on her face and said, "Let's party! Woot!"

Trish gave a weak smile and added an equally weak, "Woot!"

The woman had to do better at acting to convince anyone she was there to have fun.

Which led Lucas to believe Felina's claim. Trish couldn't be the person who'd killed Thomas Crabtree.

The killer was still out there. Now, whether the killer was the same person or people who were blackmailing Trish was another question.

They really needed a breakthrough in the case. Until then, a murderer was loose and could strike again.

Felina and Trish grabbed a table in a dark corner.

Lucas headed for a corner of the bar and ordered a beer he had no intention of drinking.

Remy arrived as Rene set the bottle of beer in

front of him. With him was former Army Ranger Beau Boyette.

Good. Beau had been a huge asset to their team when they'd worked together as mercenaries. He was an excellent marksman on a variety of weapons, highly skilled in hand-to-hand combat and a black belt in Tai Kwon Do. He'd keep Trish safe should the people blackmailing her decide to employ more physical encouragement to get their money.

Remy and Beau slipped onto stools near Lucas and ordered beers. After Rene delivered their drinks, Remy lifted his. "To keeping it real."

They touched bottles and drank.

Lucas only let the beer touch his lips before he put the bottle on the bar. "Good to see you two."

"Yeah, same. I mean, it's been what...since earlier today?" Remy grinned. "What's up?"

Keeping his face neutral, Lucas told Remy what he'd learned from Felina and Trish.

Remy slowly glanced toward the table where Felina and Trish sat. "Shelby will want to know all this. She should be here about...now."

Shelby stepped through the entrance, dressed in jeans and a white button-down blouse, tucked neatly into her waistband. Over the shirt, she wore a black leather jacket that effectively concealed the weapon Lucas was sure she had tucked into a shoulder holster.

The sheriff's deputy lifted her chin toward Remy

and headed straight for the table where Danny, the waitress, was taking Felina and Trish's orders.

"Felina said Shelby had some news." Lucas lifted his beer for another fake swallow. "Did she relay it to you?"

Remy nodded. "Facial recognition finally hit a match on the big guy who shoved Gaither into the black SUV. Johnny Lansky, also known as Big John. He's connected with the casino mafia in New Orleans. He's a prime suspect in a number of murders in and around the Big Easy. The detectives following those cases can't get enough evidence to charge the man. Witnesses disappear or end up in the morgue."

Lucas's gut clenched. "Felina witnessed him throwing Gaither into that SUV."

"All the more reason to keep her close," Remy said. "He's also suspected in a number of extortion cases. Again, no witnesses will come forward. The people they're leaning on end up in the Mississippi or a trash bin in a dark alley."

"I'm feeling better already." Lucas stared at that bottle of beer, feeling the need to down it, but knowing he couldn't. With guys like Big John too close for comfort, Lucas had to keep his wits about him. "Got any *good* news?"

"Swede looked into Thomas Crabtree's credit cards and bank accounts. He was taking out large amounts of cash and putting rooms in Baton Rouge and New Orleans on his credit cards at least once a month going back a number of years."

"Trish was a paid companion to him for only a couple of months," Lucas said.

"He was probably having affairs with other women before Trish," Remy said. "Swede also said that since Crabtree's death, there have been more large cash withdrawals from his bank accounts."

"Since he's dead, it has to be his wife removing the funds," Lucas said. "Is she the lady in green?"

Remy's brow furrowed. "Mrs. Crabtree had the motive to kill her husband. Whoever recorded that video could've been blackmailing her as well as Trish."

"She had an alibi." Lucas shook his head. "Could she have paid her gardener to say she was home at the time of the murder? That would explain the large sums of cash being siphoned out of her bank accounts. Has Swede checked into the gardener's background and bank accounts?"

Remy nodded. "He checked that first. The gardener's bank account reflects living from paycheck to paycheck. He sends money home to El Salvador every month."

"He could be hiding the cash in a jar," Beau suggested.

"He could," Remy nodded. "Or the same people who are blackmailing Trish could be blackmailing Mrs. Crabtree."

"Has anyone questioned Mrs. Crabtree yet to find out if she hired Gaither and to ask her about the cash withdrawals?"

"Not yet," Remy leaned his elbows on the bar. "When they discovered Gaither's identity, Shelby drove out to Crabtree Manor. Mrs. Crabtree wasn't there. The gardener said she'd gone to stay a night in New Orleans and would be back tomorrow."

"Do you think she made a run for it?" Lucas asked.

Remy glanced in Lucas's direction. "Shelby alerted the New Orleans Police Department to be on the lookout for her and to bring her in for questioning if they find her. We haven't heard anything from them."

"She might not have gone to New Orleans," Beau said. "She could've told the gardener that as misdirection while she heads the other way."

"Misdirection for the law or the scary people blackmailing her?" Lucas asked.

Remy's lips twisted. "Or both."

"We won't know until she turns up," Lucas said.

"In the meantime," Remy straightened, "we need to keep Trish and Marty safe from Big John."

"Do you think Mrs. Crabtree killed her husband?" Beau asked.

"If that's her in the video, yes," Remy said. "I'm ninety-nine-point-nine percent certain that the woman in the video killed Thomas Crabtree."

"If Mrs. Crabtree was that woman, her private investigator double-crossed her by recording the video of her stabbing Crabtree." Lucas tapped a finger against the beer bottle. "From what Trish said, Gaither blackmailed her first. He could have been blackmailing Mrs. Crabtree at the same time."

"Swede's still looking into Gaither's data. He's trying to get into his client files. We should be hearing from him soon."

"I would think the New Orleans Police Department would have visited Gaither's office by now," Lucas said. "Felina and I are due to go to New Orleans tomorrow. We could swing by Gaither's office."

Remy shook his head. "Now that they know it was Gaither who was killed, N.O.P.D. will have secured it for evidence gathering. You wouldn't be able to get in. If Gaither stored his files online in the cloud, Swede can access them."

"All we can do is wait until Mrs. Crabtree shows up." Lucas didn't like being held in limbo. Especially when Felina could still be in danger. She could ID Big John. From what Remy had said, Big John's witnesses never lived to testify against him.

The guys tossed around ideas over the next hour, getting no closer to any solid answers.

Beau tipped his head toward the table in the corner. "Looks like the ladies are done with their girls' night out."

"Felina and I will drop Trish at her house."

"I'll get there before her and make my way inside," Beau said. "Warn her. I'd hate for her to shoot me, thinking I'm an intruder."

"Will do," Lucas promised. "Be safe. This Big John dude sounds dangerous."

"We've gone up against worse," Beau said. "Don't worry, I'll be vigilant."

The men slid off their stools.

Beau left the bar first while Remy and Lucas waited for the women to finish hugging each other.

Shelby was the first to cross to where Remy and Lucas stood. "Are you two done chewing the fat?"

Remy dropped a kiss onto her forehead. "I never chew fat with beer." He smiled down at her. "Ready to go home?"

Shelby nodded. "I am."

He held out his arm. She slid her hand through the crook of his elbow.

Seeing them so happy together made Lucas long for the same. With Felina. Where had the battle-hardened Delta gone? The one who had thrived on adrenaline and danger?

One glance at Felina answered that question. He'd found his one and only.

"Have a good evening," Remy said to Lucas. "See you at the boat factory tomorrow?"

Lucas nodded. "I'll be there."

After Remy and Shelby left the bar, Felina and Trish joined Lucas.

"We're ready for our designated driver," Felina said with a bright smile.

Lucas's chest tightened. When you knew...you knew.

He loved this woman, and he'd do anything in his power to keep her safe.

On their way out the door, Trish paused to look at the photos nailed to the wall. "We've had some good times here, haven't we?"

"And we'll have more," Felina assured her. "Someday, we'll have our photos hanging up here."

Lucas studied the pictures of men holding trophy fish, winners of chili cooking competitions and shenanigans at an annual beer fest. "Are all these people Bayou Mambaloa residents?"

Felina nodded. "Rene likes to call this our hall of fame wall."

Lucas paused in front of a row of framed magazine covers. He read the name, Southern Home. He'd seen the house displayed on the front, and the two people standing beside it were familiar.

"Recognize them?" Felina stood beside him.

He nodded. "Brenda and Thomas Crabtree."

"That's the one year they won the Southern Home competition," Trish said. "Thomas was so proud. He'd worked so hard in his garden." She wandered further down the line of magazine covers. "Thornbridge

Manor usually wins. Missy makes sure of that. Like Thomas, she works in her garden, designing the layout, planting bulbs and annuals."

Lucas leaned closer, staring at Mrs. Crabtree's hand. The image was so small, but he could swear she wore a ring that sparkled green.

"Are you seeing what I'm seeing?" he whispered to Felina.

"It could just be the lighting," she said, moving closer, squinting at the image behind the glass protecting it.

"I'd love to be the one to talk with Mrs. Crabtree," he said.

"So would the sheriff's department and the New Orleans Police Department. We'd have to take a number." She glanced toward Trish. "Ready to go?"

Trish nodded and rejoined them.

As they left the Crawdad Hole, Felina slipped an arm around her friend. "Aren't you glad you came out?"

"Sure," Trish said. "It's always good to spend time with my friends."

Lucas chuckled as he held the door for Trish to climb into the back seat.

"Too much?" Felina asked as he held the door for her.

"No," he said and bent to kiss her. "Never too much."

Her eyes narrowed. "You're laughing at me."

"I'm enjoying being with you. Now, get in," he said, helping her up into the seat. "If we hurry, we'll have time for that third dessert."

Lucas drove slowly down Main Street, allowing enough time for Beau to reach Trish's house and get inside. If Trish was being watched, the people watching would be following them, not hanging out at Trish's house.

"I'll miss Bayou Mambaloa," Trish said. "I really liked my shop. I'd hoped to buy the building someday."

"Did you leave a light on inside your shop?" Felina turned in her seat as they passed a building with Shear Delight written on the sign.

"No," Trish said. "I try to limit the amount of electricity I use. After paying Gaither all that money I'd set aside, I could barely afford to pay the rent and utilities."

Lucas stopped and backed up.

"There's someone inside your shop with a flashlight," Felina said.

Lucas turned in the middle of the street and shined his headlights into the beauty shop's front window.

A shadowy figure knocked over a styling chair and ran toward the back of the building.

"We have to stop him," Felina cried. She flung open her door.

Lucas grabbed her arm. "Stay in the truck."

"But he's getting away," she said.

"And he might be armed," Lucas said. "Close your door and call 911."

Felina closed her door and called 911. "I'd like to report a break-in on Main Street at the Shear Delight salon. It's happening now. The guy is heading out the backdoor as we speak. Hurry."

Lucas drove around the side of the building, hoping to see where the man was heading.

As he reached the back corner, an SUV blew past him, speeding down the alleyway behind the buildings.

Lucas gunned the accelerator and gave chase. He had no intention of stopping the man but wanted to keep an eye on where he went until the sheriff's department could catch up and continue the pursuit.

The vehicle made a sharp right at the corner of a building. For a moment, Lucas lost sight of it.

"Go faster!" Felina shouted at Lucas. In her cell phone, she said, "We're following a dark SUV, headed..."

Lucas turned where the lead vehicle had turned. Ahead, the SUV took a left on Main, sliding sideways for a few feet before it straightened and shot forward.

"—east on Main," Felina continued. "He's getting away. Can't you go faster?"

Trish leaned forward. "He's heading into the curves."

Lucas did his best to keep up with the SUV, but his truck wasn't made to take curves at high speeds. Without cargo in the back, he was forced to slow at each curve or risk the truck going into a spin.

"He's getting away," Felina said.

"I can't go any faster," Lucas said. "We'll spin out and end up in a ditch, and he'll get away anyway."

When the road straightened out of the curves, the SUV was nowhere to be seen.

Lucas kept going for another mile, hoping to catch sight of the vehicle.

Felina laid a hand on his arm. "He's gone. Let's go back to the beauty shop and see what damage there is."

Lucas turned the truck around and drove back into the town, passing a sheriff's vehicle heading out. "Too late," he murmured.

Another sheriff's vehicle was parked in front of the Shear Delight, lights flashing.

Lucas, Felina and Trish got out of the truck. Trish unlocked the front door, and they stepped inside to what looked like the aftermath of a tornado. Chairs had been slashed and turned over; cabinets had been knocked over, the wood split, and the contents scattered across the floor. One of the shampoo bowls had been shattered, likely by the sledgehammer lying on the floor beside it. Red spray paint marred the walls with the words SLUT and KILLER in bold letters.

Trish pressed her hands to her cheeks. "I just can't." She turned and fell into Felina's arms.

A man in a sheriff's uniform approached through the back door. "Apparently, the perp is gone."

Lucas almost laughed. "Yeah. He headed east out of town."

"He's probably all the way to New Orleans by now."

Lucas recognized the deputy as Deputy Sarley, the man who'd responded to the break-in at Felina's apartment.

Moments later, a black pickup pulled up to the front of the shop. Remy and Shelby leaped out and hurried toward them.

"We'd just walked into the house when we heard the call on the scanner." Shelby looked around at the mess, her gaze landing on Trish. "I'm sorry this happened. Just remember, this is stuff. It can be replaced."

Trish shook her head. "No, it can't. I'd just dropped my insurance down to liability only. None of this is covered. I'm done." Her gaze went to Lucas. "Please, take me home."

"Remy and I will take photos of the damage and secure the building," Shelby said. "We'll deal with this in the morning."

Felina walked Trish back out to the truck. Lucas helped her into the back seat and closed the door.

Felina wrapped her arms around Lucas's waist.

"She's going to give up. How many times can a person be knocked down before they don't get up again?"

"She'll make it through this. She has you, Shelby, and the wonderful people of Bayou Mambaloa. Everything will turn out all right."

"I hope you're right," she said.

Lucas opened the passenger door, handed Felina up into her seat and rounded the front of the truck to slide into the driver's seat.

Felina turned sideways in her seat, looking back at her friend. "Trish, do you want to stay with me tonight?"

Trish shook her head. "No. I want to be alone. I have a lot of thinking to do."

"About that," Lucas said. "Remy positioned, Beau, one of the Brotherhood Protectors inside your home. With all the break-ins and threats, we felt it necessary to have someone with you."

"Why?" She leaned her head back and closed her eyes. "I have nothing left to give."

"I'm going to stay with you tonight," Felina declared. "You shouldn't be alone."

Trish laughed. "You just told me there'd be a man in my house. "I won't be alone. No. Please. Don't stay with me tonight. Let me wallow in my self-pity by myself."

Felina bit her bottom lip. "I'm not comfortable with that."

"I'm beginning to believe this is Karma coming back to bite me in the ass." She held up her hand. "Don't worry. I won't do anything rash. I promise."

Felina exchanged a look with Lucas.

He could tell she wanted to stay with her friend, but Trish wasn't having it.

When they pulled up in front of Trish's cottage, two more vehicles were parked beside Trish's four-door sedan.

"Is someone having a party at my house and forgot to invite me?"

Lucas dropped down from his seat and came around the truck to help Trish down.

She'd just gotten her feet on the ground when the front door opened, and Marty stepped out, followed by Rafael "Romeo" Romero.

Trish let out a choked sob and buried her face in her hands. "Why is he here?" she said between sobs. "Tell him to go away. I c-can't marry him. He deserves someone better."

Marty hurried toward her. "Hey. What's all this? Why the tears?"

"Go away," Trish said, her words muffled against her palms.

"I'm not going anywhere," he said. "Not without you." He scooped her up into his arms and held her close.

Trish wrapped her arms around his neck and shook with the force of her sobs.

"Shh," Marty soothed. "Everything is going to be all right."

"No, it's not," she said into his shirt. "You can't marry me. I'll ruin your life."

"Sweetheart, even though we haven't said the vows yet, I'm all in with you. For better or worse. We'll figure it out together."

Felina climbed down from the truck and wrapped her arm around Lucas's waist.

He held her close while Marty tried to calm Trish.

"I should've told you everything," Trish said. "But I was afraid you'd change your mind...about us."

"Nothing will change my mind about us," he said. "Beau and Romeo filled me in on what's been happening. I wish I'd known sooner. We could've figured out something before this. You've been carrying this burden by yourself for too long. Let me help."

She looked up at him with tears running down her cheeks. "And if I go to jail?"

"We'll hire the best lawyer." He looked over Trish's head at Lucas and Felina. "Thank you for bringing her home. I'll take care of her now. I should've been taking care of her all along." He kissed the top of her head. "I love you, Trish. I'll do everything in my power to make things better."

"Beau and Romeo will stand guard tonight," Lucas said. "We'll figure out where to go from here tomorrow."

Marty nodded. "Thank you." His gaze went to Felina. "And thank you for being there for her. You're a good friend."

"Take good care of her," Felina said. "Don't break her heart."

"I won't," he said.

Once Marty and Trish were safely inside the cottage, with Beau and Romeo there to provide protection, Lucas held the door for Felina.

She climbed in and buckled her seatbelt.

Lucas slid into the driver's seat and backed out of the driveway.

"I'm glad Trish has Marty," she said softly. "I think they'll make it as a couple."

"No regrets?" Lucas asked.

Felina shook her head. "None."

Lucas smiled. Felina was completely free of her prior relationship, which left her open to possibilities. He wanted to be that possibility. No. He wanted to be more than a possibility.

He shifted into drive and pulled out onto the road. "Home?"

Felina hesitated for a moment, a frown pulling at her eyebrows. "No."

He cast a glance her way, a sense of trepidation washing over him at the determined set of her chin. "Where to?'

She stared straight ahead. "Crabtree Manor."

CHAPTER 13

Lucas drove through town and out into the country. "What's the plan?"

"I'm not exactly sure," Felina said. The idea to go to Crabtree Manor was the culmination of several images and sound bites she'd seen or heard throughout the day.

"Shelby said the gardener informed her that Mrs. Crabtree was in New Orleans for the night."

Felina nodded. "I understand."

"She won't be there for us to ask questions," Lucas continued.

"Which is part of the reason I want to go now." She glanced at Lucas. "You could drop me off at the beginning of her driveway. I can go in alone. That way, if I'm caught, I'll be the only one charged with trespassing."

His brow furrowed. "You know people can shoot you for trespassing, don't you?"

She nodded. "Thus, the reason why I want to go while Mrs. Crabtree is away."

"What if she has a security system?" he asked.

"I didn't see one when we were there. Nor did I see security cameras."

"Let me get this straight. You plan on going into her house?"

Felina nodded. "By myself. I don't want you to come with me."

He shook his head. "Sweetheart, where you go, I go."

"Seriously, I'm going alone," she said. "I don't want you to go to jail because of me."

"And I don't want you to get shot." Lucas slowed to take a curve. "She could have come home early."

"I'll check for her car in the garage before I go in."

"And how do you propose to get in?"

She shrugged. "I'll check for windows that weren't locked. There has to be at least one."

"And if you don't find one unlocked, can we go home and forget about committing a felony?"

She sighed. "Yes."

"What are you looking for if you get inside Crabtree Manor?"

"The ring," she said. "And maybe, the costume."

"If Mrs. Crabtree was the woman in green who killed Thomas Crabtree, don't you think she would've gotten rid of the costume by now? She probably ditched it that same day in New Orleans, where it was buried under the mountains of trash generated during Mardi Gras."

Felina had thought that as well. "I don't know why, but I feel compelled to look for something—*anything* that either confirms she was the one or completely exonerates her." She faced Lucas. "When I went to Trish's house, I found the blue dress and mask."

"Trish had nothing to hide," Lucas reminded her. "She didn't kill Mr. Crabtree. You said so yourself."

Felina nodded. "I one-hundred-percent believe that to be true. Yet, Big John, or whoever it is, is blackmailing her with damning photographs. What if they're doing the same to Mrs. Crabtree? They could be extorting money from her, using the same threat they used with Trish."

"Except Mrs. Crabtree could be that woman in green. We should let the sheriff's department question her and search her house for evidence."

"They did immediately after her husband's death. But they didn't know what to look for."

"The green dress and mask?" His lips pressed together. "Again, she'd be insane to keep those."

"True," Felina said. "Someone might've seen her in the costume, but they might not have noticed the ring."

"It seems like a long shot." Lucas slowed as they

approached the gate to Crabtree Manor. "I don't like this plan."

"Then leave me here. I'll find my way back to town."

"Not an option." He passed the gate.

Felina swiveled in her seat. "You passed her gate."

"Yes, I did. I'm not parking anywhere near it. What kind of covert operation would it be if I left my truck where anyone would notice it?" A quarter mile past the Crabtree Manor gate, Lucas pulled off the paved road onto a gravel road and drove his truck into the woods, circling so that the truck faced the road but was hidden behind a tangle of briar bushes.

Lucas turned off the engine. "Are you sure you want to do this?"

"Yes," she said. "Have you ever acted on a gut feeling?"

Lucas drew in a deep breath and let it out slowly. "I have. A number of times."

"Was your gut right?"

"Every damned time," he admitted.

She pressed a hand to her belly. "My gut's telling me to do this."

"Mine isn't," he countered.

She looked at him in the starlight filtering through the trees and windshield. "Is your gut telling you this is a bad idea?"

He stared into her eyes for a long moment, then answered, "No. Come on. Let's do this and get back home. The sheriff's department will question her tomorrow."

He reached into the console for his gun and a flashlight.

Felina slipped the knife Lucas had given her out of her purse and hooked the sheath onto the waistband of her jeans.

Lucas slid out of his seat and then dropped to the ground. Before he could go around to help Felina out, she climbed down from her seat and hurried to meet him at the front of the truck.

"As long as there isn't any traffic, we'll follow the road," he said. "I don't want to get lost in the woods and spend the rest of the night finding our way back to the truck."

Lucas led the way, walking along the gravel road and then the paved road.

Thankfully, no other vehicles passed, and they were saved from hiding in the ditch with the snakes and alligators native to the bayou.

Felina shivered at the thought of stepping on a snake. She didn't dare think about coming face-to-face with an alligator.

When they came within sight of the brick and wrought iron gate, he stopped short and studied the fence. As impressive as the gate was, it only kept vehicles from driving onto the property; the rest of the fence surrounding the property was made of metal pipes welded together. All they had to do was easily climb over or duck through it.

Felina ducked through, glad it wasn't barbed wire or a massive stone wall they would have had to scale.

Once on the other side, Lucas avoided the open, manicured lawns and kept to the tree line and shadows.

Felina followed, doing what he did. When they reached the clearing where the house sat bathed in moonlight, Lucas stopped in the shadows.

Felina came to stand beside him.

Not a single light shone through the windows.

Felina was mildly relieved. If Mrs. Crabtree was home, surely, she would have left a light on in a hallway in case she needed to move around at night.

"The front is too open," Lucas said. "We'll approach from the rear."

Again, Felina followed Lucas.

Again, he kept to the tree line, making a wide circle around the house until they were directly behind it. The garage was separate from the house, with four overhead doors.

Lucas eased up to one of the windows on the side and peered inside. "How many cars should be in here?"

"I don't know," Felina said.

"Do you know what kind of car Mrs. Crabtree normally drives?"

"A white expensive sports car." She moved up

beside him and peered through the window. Low light glowed inside the garage just enough for her to make out the vehicles within. A white crew cab pickup occupied the farthest bay. "The truck was Mr. Crabtree's. I'm surprised she hasn't sold it yet."

A sporty four-wheel-drive red Jeep was parked beside the truck. "The Jeep was also Mr. Crabtree's."

Closest to the door stood an antique Model T Ford. "Mr. Crabtree drove the Model T in the town's parades." She straightened. "Mrs. Crabtree's car isn't here."

"Okay, let's look for that window that isn't locked." He walked to the corner of the garage closest to the house, looked both ways and then ran across the open concrete drive and the lawn to the porch.

Felina didn't understand why they had to run. Mrs. Crabtree wasn't home. Still, she did exactly what Lucas had, arriving at the porch only slightly winded. They climbed the steps to the wide ground-floor porch wrapped around the house on all four sides.

Lucas started at the corner, trying to slide the windows up, testing them one at a time.

Felina tried the one closest to the back door. It didn't budge.

Her gaze went to the door. What were the chances that the back door was unlocked? Probably nil. She walked to the door and twisted the handle. The door opened.

"Uh, Lucas," she whispered.

He looked up from the window he was trying to open and frowned. "Really?"

She shrugged. "Yeah." Felina waited until Lucas joined her before she entered the house. "It's not breaking and entering if the door's unlocked, right?"

"Still breaking and entering," he said so softly she barely heard the words.

Now that she was inside the house, the task of searching for the costume was a little overwhelming. With all the rooms, closets and cabinets, they could be there all night.

On the other hand, the ring's location should be easier to guess. It would be somewhere in the master bedroom, tucked into a jewelry box or drawer.

"You want to look for the costume in the closets or basement?" she suggested.

"Only if that's where you're going," he said, switching on his flashlight with a red lens cover. "We stick together, or we leave now."

A shiver of apprehension slithered down Felina's spine. Sticking together was fine by her. "Let's start in the master bedroom." She led the way up the stairs, glad she'd visited the house recently and knew exactly where to go. She climbed the sweeping staircase, turned right at the top and walked to the door at the end of the hall.

Even though she knew Mrs. Crabtree wasn't

home, she stepped aside and let Lucas ease the door open to check inside before allowing her to enter.

The room was as she'd seen it the last time she'd been there, only darker, with only starlight shining through the window to guide her way.

Since Lucas had the only flashlight, she directed him. "We're looking for a jewelry box or cabinet."

Lucas shined the red light around the room, pausing over the dresser. They moved toward the antique and studied the mirrored tray in the middle. On it was a silver hairbrush and comb. No jewelry.

Lucas crossed the carpet to one of the nightstands on either side of the massive four-poster bed. They looked in every drawer, finding tissues, sleeping masks and several bottles of sleep aids. No jewelry. The other nightstand yielded a couple of books on historical figures of the eighteen hundreds, reading glasses and nasal strips for chronic snoring.

Lucas checked under the bed, then headed for one of the other two doors. The one on the right led into the bathroom. After checking all the drawers, with no luck, they moved to the other door.

This one led into a large room lined with shelves for shoes and purses and rods full of hanging clothes.

Lucas closed the door and turned on the light, making it much easier to see than using a red-lensed flashlight.

On the far wall were built-in drawers too shallow for clothes but perfect for jewelry. Felina hurried forward and tried to pull on the handles of the top drawer. It didn't budge.

Lucas pointed to a brass fixture above the top drawer. "It needs a key."

Felina's heart sank. To come this far, find the jewelry box and be stumped by the lack of a key, how unfair was that?

Then she tried to think like the woman whose jewelry was locked in the drawers in front of her.

"I can't imagine a woman carrying a set of keys around her bedroom," Felina said. "She'd want instant access to her accessories without having to search too far for the key." Felina ran her hands across the top of the cabinet and down the sides. No luck.

"Could this be it?" Lucas pointed to a hook on the wall beside the light switch. A single key hung from a bejeweled keychain.

He handed the keychain to Felina.

She fitted the key into the lock and turned it.

When she tried the top drawer again, it opened easily to display a couple dozen rings with various stones and settings. Not one of them was the emerald ring Felina had seen in the video worn by the woman who'd murdered Thomas Crabtree.

She closed the top drawer and opened the next one. This drawer held bracelets. The next one had necklaces. The fourth drawer had even more necklaces. The fifth drawer held neatly folded scarves, and the bottom drawer held neckties.

No emerald ring.

"Where else would she store rings?" Lucas asked.

"It would be here." Felina sighed. "I guess we should look for the costume. We can give it another thirty minutes, then we can leave."

Lucas reached for the door handle and froze.

"What?" Felina whispered, straining to hear what Lucas must have heard.

He motioned for her to slip behind the rack of formal gowns. As she did, he backed behind a rack of men's suits, moving a couple of suitcases in front of his legs. Then he reached out and flipped the light switch off.

A door creaked open in the master bedroom.

Felina's breath caught and held as she strained to hear the sound of footsteps moving around the room. Drawers were opened and closed. The footsteps moved into the bathroom, clicking across the tile. More drawers opened and closed, the sounds echoing against the tile floors and shower walls. Then, the footsteps moved out of the bathroom and stopped in front of the walk-in closet door.

Her heart hammering against her ribs, Felina watched as the door opened. A slender hand reached inside and flipped on the light.

That's when Felina realized she'd left the key with the bejeweled keychain in the lock.

A hand reached into the closet, grabbed a suitcase and dragged it into the other room.

A moment later, the hand reached in again for another case and dragged it out, leaving Lucas's legs exposed beneath the line of suits hanging down to below his waist.

For a couple of minutes, the noises coming from the bedroom were little more than the rustle of fabric. Felina could picture a suitcase being packed with clothes.

Footsteps moved toward the closet again. The door opened wider, and Brenda Crabtree entered and walked to a rack of blouses. She yanked half a dozen from their hangers and rushed back into the bedroom. A moment later, she was back in the closet, standing in front of the row of pants. Again, she yanked several from their hangers, turned and started for the door.

A pair of trousers slipped from her collection and dropped to the floor. She bent to pick them up and froze, her eyes narrowed and then she uttered a curse and fell backward in her mad scramble to get away.

Lucas parted the row of suits and stepped into the open. "Mrs. Crabtree, I'm not going to hurt you."

"You!" She clutched her trousers to her chest like a shield. "What are you doing in my closet? Are you here to steal from me? Go ahead. Take what you want. I don't care. You can have it all. Just leave me alone."

"I'm not here to take anything." Lucas held out his hand. "Let me help you up."

She scooted even further back, shaking her head. "No, please. Take everything; just don't hurt me."

"I'm not going to hurt you." He backed away, leaving a clear path for her to leave the closet. "You're free to go."

"It's a trick," she said. "You're with them, aren't you? I told them I'd sell the manor. All they have to do is bring me the papers. I'll sign. You don't have to threaten me. I hate this place. I just want to leave and never come back to Louisiana. Please, I'll sign anything. Just let me go."

Felina's heart hurt at the desperation in Mrs. Crabtree's tone. It was the same desperation Trish had displayed. Felina started to part the long dresses.

Lucas gave a sharp but almost imperceptible shake of his head, visible only to her. She stilled and waited to see what would happen, wishing she hadn't gotten Lucas into this mess.

If she wanted, Mrs. Crabtree could have Lucas arrested for trespassing.

"Ma'am," Lucas tried again. "I'm not going to hurt you."

Crabtree looked up at him, her eyes narrowing. "You aren't? They didn't send you?"

"They...who?" Lucas asked.

"The men who've been extorting money out of

me for the past six months, threatening to turn me over to the police for murdering my husband."

Brenda Crabtree struggled to stand. When she was up and steady, she lifted her chin. "Well, you can tell them I'm done. If they want me to sign the property over to them, they'd better do it now because I'm leaving, one way or another."

"I don't want your property. I'm not going to threaten you."

"Then why are you here?"

"I'm looking for an emerald ring. I saw it in a photograph of you on the wall of fame at the Crawdad Hole Bar and Grill."

"You broke into my house for an emerald ring?" The older woman shook her head. "I could have you arrested for trespassing, breaking and entering and assault. Why would you do such a thing?"

"Locating that ring is important to me," he said.

Felina closed her eyes. The man was up to his eyeballs in trouble, and he was still trying to find the ring.

"I don't know what ring you're talking about," she said. "I don't even care. Get out of my house before I call the sheriff."

"Ma'am, I'm sorry I've bothered you, but it's imperative that I find that ring. Do you own such a ring? It's got a square stone and has little diamonds on either side of the main setting."

Brenda Crabtree studied Lucas as though she didn't trust him or anything he had to say. "I had an emerald ring similar to what you just described," she said. "I gave it to a friend. Why do you care so much about that ring?"

"You gave it to a friend?" Lucas persisted. "What friend?"

"Me," a female voice said. "I'm the friend."

Hidden behind the rack of formals, Felina could only see a small section of the closet in front of her, including Mrs. Crabtree's face. She could not see who was in the master bedroom, but the voice was familiar.

"Brenda, come out of the closet," the woman said. "What are you doing in there anyway?'"

Brenda eased past Lucas and out of the closet.

Lucas followed Mrs. Crabtree into the master bedroom.

Felina fought the urge to step out as well, but Lucas didn't want her to let Mrs. Crabtree know she was there. She stayed hidden. Listening, ready to jump out if Lucas needed her.

"Missy, what are you doing here?" Mrs. Crabtree asked.

"I came to check on you," Missy said. "Is this man harassing you?"

"How did you get into my house?" Mrs. Crabtree asked.

"The door was unlocked," Missy said. "I was

worried about you and came up to see if you were all right."

"I'm fine," Mrs. Crabtree said. "This man was helping me find something. He was just leaving."

"Are you leaving, too?" Missy asked. "These are your suitcases and clothes, aren't they?"

"Yes. I'm going on a little vacation," Mrs. Crabtree said.

"I'm afraid that isn't possible," Missy's voice grew colder. "You see, I know where you went today."

"Of course, you do." Mrs. Crabtree said. "I went to New Orleans. I told the gardener where I was going."

"You went to the Historical Society, didn't you?" Missy's voice was harsh.

"Yes, I did," Mrs. Crabtree said. "I made a donation in my husband's name."

"And what was that donation, Brenda?" Missy's voice was tight. "What did you give them?"

"I gave them this house and everything in it," Mrs. Crabtree said.

"Bitch!" Missy screamed. "You were supposed to sell it to CEI. You had six months. Six damn months to sell it. They gave you the best offer. I told them you'd sell it to them. It was part of the deal. You have to tell the Historical Society you changed your mind."

"I can't," Mrs. Crabtree said. "All the papers have been signed and recorded at the courthouse. The house and land belong to them now."

"You have no idea what you've done," Missy cried. "No idea."

"CEI is run by a bunch of crooks. They would have torn down Crabtree Manor and put a casino in its place," Mrs. Crabtree said. "I couldn't let that happen, no matter how much they threatened me."

"You hated Thomas. You said you wished he'd die. Hell, he cheated on you so many times. Even *I* had an affair with him, right under your nose. Then he dumped me for that twit, Trish. A child!"

"I know," Mrs. Crabtree said. "He told me all of it when I showed him the photos my private investigator took of him with you and with Trish. I asked for a divorce, and he threw the prenup agreement in my face. I'd signed it back when I was young, stupid and thought I was in love. I had no choice but to stay in this cesspool of a state, in a farce of a marriage to a man who didn't give two shits about me."

"Then why didn't you sell this place to CEI?" Missy asked. "It would've had Thomas rolling over in his grave. You'd have had your revenge."

"I might have sold to CEI, but I resented being told what I could and couldn't do. I'd spent my marriage letting Thomas walk all over me because he basically owned me. I had no career to fall back on and no higher education. I couldn't support myself without him. He knew it. He did whatever the hell he wanted, and I was stuck. After Thomas was murdered and Gaither started blackmailing me, it was Thomas all over again. Once again, I had no control over my life. Decisions were being forced on me. I'd reached the point that I'd had enough. I didn't care if I lived or died. I wanted out."

"Yeah, well, you're going to get your wish," Missy said. "Those threats you were receiving were real. The people dishing out the consequences don't care that your ex-husband hurt your feelings. They care that you cheated them out of the land they needed to build a casino in this parish. Big John had a huge stake in the sale to CEI. He stood to make tens of thousands of dollars in commissions for facilitating the sale."

"You mean coercing the sale," Mrs. Crabtree said.

"They gave you multiple chances," Missy said. "I got Thomas out of the way."

Felina swallowed a gasp. Missy was the woman in green? She killed Thomas?

CHAPTER 14

HOLY SHIT! Never in a million years would Felina have guessed Missy was the murderer. Sure, the woman was crazy...but deadly?

Wow.

Felina wished she had a gun. Then she remembered the knife she'd hooked onto her jeans. It wasn't enough.

"Now, your most pressing problem is that Big John never leaves loose ends," Missy said. "He'll be around to collect what you cheated him out of."

Mrs. Crabtree said, "I have nothing left to lose."

"You're wrong," Missy said. "There's the matter of your life. Big John will collect on it."

"I'll be waiting for him."

"You don't have to wait long," a deep voice said from the master bedroom.

Felina pressed a hand to her chest to keep her heart from leaping out.

"Don't reach for your weapon, or I'll be forced to shoot the old woman," Big John said. "That's right, lay it on the floor, nice and easy."

"Let Mrs. Crabtree go," Lucas said. "Killing her won't buy you anything."

"You're wrong. The fact she gave the home and property away gives me a black mark with my employer. I have zero tolerance for black marks and liars."

A shot went off. Felina clapped her hand over her mouth to keep from crying out.

"He's down. Get his gun."

Felina's breath lodged in her throat. She knew in her heart Lucas was the man down. Every muscle in her body screamed to move. To check on Lucas and call for an ambulance. Yet, she held back, knowing that if she emerged from the closet at that moment, she'd be shot, too. Then who would rescue the others after Big John and his thugs left?

"Secure their wrists and ankles," Big John said.

"What are you doing? You can't be serious," Missy said. "We're on the same side."

"You failed to get the property for my boss," Big John said. "We have no need for your services, which makes you yet another loose end to be eliminated."

"But I got Thomas out of the way for you," Missy said.

"For what? Your way didn't work," Big John said. "Now, it's our way. The Historical Society will have no need for this property if there's nothing on it left to preserve."

"What are you going to do?" Mrs. Crabtree asked.

"Remove the historical significance and tie up loose ends in the process."

"You can't do that," Missy screamed. "That's murder."

"How's that feel when the shoe's on the other foot?" Big John said. "Enjoy the last minutes of your life." A door closed in the other room.

"I'm going to die," Missy sobbed. "Who's going to carry on the tradition at Thornbridge Manor? We would have won this year. Nothing could stop us."

Felina listened for any indication that Big John was still in the other room. She eased out from behind the formal gowns and peered around the closet door.

Only three people were in the master bedroom. Mrs. Crabtree, Missy Thornbridge and Lucas.

Felina's heart leaped into her throat. She ran to Lucas and knelt beside him, feeling for a pulse. She almost cried with relief.

"Felina. Sweet Jesus, we're saved. Where did you come from?" Missy called out.

"Shh, Missy," Mrs. Crabtree whispered. "Don't let Big John hear you."

"Untie us, Felina," Missy hissed. "You have to free

us before Big John burns Crabtree Manor to the ground."

Felina pulled her knife from the sheath and sliced through the zip ties securing Lucas's wrists and ankles. Then she rolled him onto his back, searching for wounds. She found one near his right shoulder and pressed her hand into it to stem the flow of blood. "Lucas. Sweetheart. You have to wake up."

"When the bullet hit him, he staggered backward," Mrs. Crabtree said. "He tripped on the rug and hit his head on the corner of the four-poster bed."

Felina felt the back of Lucas's head, finding a knot the size of a goose egg.

"Felina, don't waste your time on him. He's dead," Missy said. "Untie us."

Lucas wasn't dead. His pulse was strong; he just wasn't waking up. "Lucas, baby, you have to wake up."

"For the love of Pete," Missy cursed. "Untie us at once."

Felina left Lucas, crossed to Mrs. Crabtree and cut the zip ties from her wrists and ankles.

Mrs. Crabtree wrapped an arm around Felina. "I know I don't deserve your kindness but thank you from the bottom of my heart."

Felina handed Mrs. Crabtree the knife and went back to help Lucas.

Mrs. Crabtree knelt beside Missy, where she lay

on her side on the floor. "Missy, did you kill Thomas?"

"Of course, I did. And no need to thank me," Missy said. "The bastard deserved to die. He dumped me for a goddamn child."

Felina wasn't too surprised to learn that the green lady was, in fact, Missy Thornbridge. The woman was notorious for taking competition too far.

Felina cupped Lucas's cheek. "Lucas, you have to wake up. They're going to burn the place down. I can't carry you out of here. You need to wake up and walk your ass out on your own steam." She brushed a kiss across his lips. "Please, Lucas, you have to wake up."

Lucas stirred beneath her. His eyelids blinked open, and he stared up into hers. "Hey," he said.

"Hey, yourself," she said. "Can you move?"

He shifted his arms and legs. "I think so."

"Then let's get moving." Felina held out a hand.

Lucas grasped it. She pulled him slowly to his feet and stood close while he got his balance.

"Where did Big John go?" he asked.

"Out of here. That's all I know," Felina said. "I think they're going to burn this old house to the ground."

Lucas headed for the door, opened it and stepped out into the hallway.

Felina hurried after him. As she passed Mrs. Crabtree, the woman held up the knife.

"You might need this," she said.

Felina slid the knife into the sheath at her waist and hurried to catch up to Lucas. "Where are you going?" she asked.

"We need to stop Big John before he lights the match."

Lucas fought for focus. The gunshot wound must have hit in a place that caused only minimal damage. He moved through the big house, searching for Big John and his assistant.

He found them outside on the porch, sloshing fuel across the wooden decking. He had the element of surprise with him. They would think he was still tied up in the master bedroom.

Big John hadn't known anyone else was in that closet. Lucas was proud and thankful that Felina had remained in hiding until Big John and his partner had left them alone.

At first groggy, Lucas kept moving until his brain cleared. He hurried to a side entrance and stepped out onto the deck. Half-jogging, he headed for the front, where he hoped to stop Big John and his cohort from setting the house on fire.

As he rounded the corner, Big John was coming from the opposite direction.

Lucas was ready. He bent and drove his shoulder into Big John's gut, not stopping until the man flipped over the railing and landed hard on the lawn.

Felina raced out to the man lying still on the

grass. She tugged and pulled the zip ties out of Big John's back pocket and used them to secure the man's ankles. She was looping the plastic strip around the big guy's wrists when he stirred.

Seconds later, he grabbed Felina's hair and yanked her backward and into his lap.

"Let go of me," she cried.

"No way," Big John said. "You're my ticket out of here."

Lucas dealt with the other guy, slamming his head into a wall. The man fell to the deck unconscious, and Lucas took his gun.

Lucas stared out at the lawn where he'd sent Big John, and his heart clenched.

Felina gave him a tight smile. "I've got everything under control."

No, she didn't. John had her in his grip. He was big enough he could snap her neck with very little effort.

"Let her go, Big John," Lucas pointed the gun at the bastard. "This show is over." Though he aimed at the big man, Lucas couldn't pull the trigger without hitting Felina.

"Not quite over," Big John said. "Cue my grand exit with your pretty girlfriend."

"I'm not going with you," Felina said.

Big John pressed the barrel of his pistol to her temple. "Oh, I think you are."

"You're not listening," Felina said.

"Perhaps you're the one who isn't listening," Big John said.

"Lucas are you going to let this asshat tell me what to do?" she called out.

"No, ma'am," he responded evenly, his gaze on her hand pulling the knife from its sheath.

He braced himself, his aim on the big guy.

Felina jammed the knife into Big John's thigh, then ducked and rolled onto the ground.

Lucas pulled the trigger. The bullet hit Big John in the heart. For a long moment, the man's eyes rounded. Then he slumped sideways in the grass.

Felina leaped to her feet and threw herself into Lucas's arms. "I don't *ever* want to have to wait in a closet while you're being shot—*ever again*."

He held her, his shoulder aching, but he didn't care. He had Felina in his arms, and Big John was dead and wouldn't terrorize or blackmail another soul.

He brushed the hair from Felina's face and kissed her. "You might not be ready to hear this, but I have to say it. I love you, Felina. I think I've loved you from the first time I saw you helping an old man put flowers for his wife into his car. You're kind, caring and a good friend to just about every-body. And you're beautiful, sexy and an amazing lover. Please give me the chance to convince you that I'm sincere in my love and that I'm also the one for you."

She touched a finger to his lips. "Slow down, cowboy."

He kissed her finger and waited for her to speak.

"First of all…I know," she said.

He gave her a crooked smile. "You know what?"

Her answering smile melted his insides. "I know what I know, and that's just that I love you, Lucas."

His heart filled with so much joy he thought it might explode. "How do you know?"

Her grin broadened. "I want to spend every waking and sleeping minute with you. Yours is the first face I want to see in the morning and the last one I want to see at night. I don't like being away from you. I count the seconds until we're together again. I like your corny pickup lines and the way you hold me." She wrapped her arms around his neck. "Take me home and make love to me."

"Third dessert?" he murmured, nuzzling her ear.

"Fourth and fifth, if you're up to it after a visit to the ER."

"I'll be up to it. And I have some more pickup lines to try out on you."

She pressed a kiss to his lips. "I can't wait."

"You'll have to wait until the sheriff gets here to take your statements and book Thomas's murderer," Mrs. Crabtree called out. "They're on their way."

Lucas and Felina turned to find Mrs. Crabtree standing on the porch with Missy Thornbridge. The murderer's hands were still bound in a zip tie.

"Please, reconsider," Missy said. "At least wait to turn me in until after Colonial Day. I've worked so hard. I know Thornbridge Manor will win this year."

"You killed a man," Mrs. Crabtree reminded her.

"So?" Missy said. "Nobody misses him."

"Why did you kill him?" Mrs. Crabtree asked. "Was it revenge because he dumped you?"

"Oh, hell no. I got over that. I only slept with him to learn his secrets about Crabtree Manor."

"Is it all about our estates?" Mrs. Crabtree shook her head. "No house is worth killing over."

"You don't understand. You never loved Crabtree Manor like I love Thornbridge. It's my life, my blood. My love. I'd do anything for her."

"Even kill?"

"Thomas wouldn't sell. I knew with him out of the way, you'd sell to the first big developer, and they'd tear the house down and put up a resort. But you didn't sell right away. I had to move it along. Framing you for murder was a brilliant way to make you spend all your money paying the extortion fees. Then you'd have to sell to the highest bidder."

"You did all that to get me to sell?" Mrs. Crabtree shook her head. "No matter how much I hated living here, I couldn't let developers destroy the building. I didn't donate the property to the historical society for Thomas. I did it for me. It helped me lay my anger to rest. Now, I can leave with a free heart and conscience."

"Where will you go?" Felina asked.

The older woman smiled. "I bought a condo on the outer banks in North Carolina. I was going to leave in the morning to get away from Big John's extortion and threats."

"Now that Missy's confessed and Big John's dead, he can't threaten you anymore," Lucas said.

"Good riddance," Mrs. Crabtree said. "I'm still leaving, but I'll take a few more days to pack everything I want and donate everything else."

Lights flashed on top of the two sheriff's vehicles coming up the driveway, followed by an ambulance.

Lucas slipped an arm around Felina and pulled her up against him. "Think they'll give us a ride to my truck?"

She nodded. "We just have to ask."

"After all this excitement, will you find it hard to return to our normal, boring lives?" Lucas asked.

Felina chuckled. "Are you kidding? There's nothing boring about being the only florist in Bayou Mambaloa, especially with Colonial Day and a wedding coming up sooner than you think. And I haven't placed orders yet."

Lucas stared up at the star-studded sky and smiled. "I'm gonna love this town."

Felina sighed. "It is a wonderful place to live."

"Any place you are is a wonderful place to live," Lucas said. "You're like a bunch of forget-me-nots, etched in my mind forever."

She leaned into him. "That's a good one."

EPILOGUE

"FELINA!" Trish hurried toward Felina, careful not to trip on the train of her wedding gown. "You've completely outdone yourself. I love you so very much. Thank you for being my best friend and the sister I never had."

Felina carefully hugged the beautiful bride. "I'm glad you like everything. We've been at it since the wee hours of the morning to get everything in place. Especially the floral arch."

"It was so nice of the entire town, pitching in to fix up my shop and adding to the floral decorations. Our town is the absolute best."

"Yes, it is," Felina agreed.

"Who did you get to help with all this?" Trish shook her head, looking around the room in awe.

"Lucas, of course, and Bernie, Shelby, Danny, Gisele, Camille and..." Felina laughed. "It might be easier to ask who didn't help. They were the same folks who helped on Colonial Day getting Crabtree Manor ready for visitors and the Historical Society."

"You did Crabtree Manor proud. I never saw Mrs. Crabtree so happy as when she handed over the key."

Felina grinned. "She offloaded a huge burden."

"Yes, she did. And look at this," Trish said. "Everything today is perfect." She waved at the vases of flowers around the room where she had spent the morning with a makeup artist and a hairstylist. Her hair was pulled up in a sophisticated updo with loose ringlets framing her face.

Felina's heart swelled at her friend's beauty. "You're stunning," she said. "Marty is a lucky man."

"I'm a lucky woman," Trish said, her cheeks flushing a pretty pink. "He's been so kind and attentive. I can't wait to spend the rest of my life with him."

After one more glance around, Felina turned toward the exit. "I'd better go find my seat. It's about that time."

"Felina…" Trish stopped her before she reached the door. "Thank you for understanding about me and Marty and for not giving up on our friendship. It means more to me than you can ever know."

Felina reached for Trish's hand. "You two were meant to be together. How could I be anything but happy for you both?"

Trish's eyes filled. "And just think…if I hadn't

stolen Marty from you, you would never have found Lucas."

Felina stared down at the engagement ring on her left hand, still amazed at how full her heart was.

"I was surprised he proposed so soon," Trish said. "And even more surprised you said yes."

Felina lifted a shoulder and let it fall, happiness filling every part of her being. "Well, when you know he's the one for you...you know."

BEAU

BAYOU BROTHERHOOD PROTECTORS
BOOK #4

New York Times & USA Today
Bestselling Author

ELLE JAMES

BEAU

Bayou
BROTHERHOOD PROTECTORS

New York Times & USA Today Bestselling Author
ELLE JAMES

CHAPTER 1

BEAU BOYETTE PULLED into the parking lot at the Gautreaux Chateau on the bayou west of New Orleans, Louisiana. Dressed in a Robin Hood costume, complete with a green coat, a quiver of arrows, a thick belt and the signature green hat, he felt ridiculous, mostly because of the goddamn green tights. He prayed his Brotherhood Protectors teammates hadn't seen him leaving the boarding house in Bayou Mambaloa. He'd never hear the end of it.

He dug into his jacket pocket for his cell phone. Having put off this call as long as he could, he needed to get it over with and clear his slate for however long his mission might take.

"Beau, *cher*," his mother, Josephine Boyette, answered on the first ring in her heavy Cajun accent. "*Comment ça se plume?*" Translated: How's it plucking?

Beau grinned at his mother's favorite Cajun saying. *"Bien, Maman."*

"Why we have non seen you in da past week? You're gonna be here for da Sunday dinner, *oui*? It will be da first time in eight years since all ten of *mes enfants* have been together."

"Maman, I can't make the family dinner on Sunday. I got my first assignment and have to work."

"You no can put it off 'til Monday?" she asked.

"No, *Maman*," he said. "I work 24/7."

"You no in *l'armee* anymore. You come to da dinner."

"No, *Maman*. I'm not in the Army anymore, but I work providing protection for people," he explained for the fifth time since hiring on with the Brotherhood Protectors.

"Surely, you get a day off," his mother said. "Do I need to talk to da boss?"

God forbid his mother should talk to his lead over the Bayou Brotherhood Protectors. He'd never hear the end of the ribbing he'd get from Remy Montagne or the rest of the team. Or she could make it worse and take her complaint to Hank Patterson, the man who'd started the original Brotherhood Protectors organization.

Beau sighed. *"Maman*, you don't need to talk to my boss. I signed on to dis job, knowing it could mean working 24/7 to protect our clients. I'm just calling to let you know I won't be at da family dinner. I'll try to make it another time."

"But—" his mother started.

"Je suis désolé," Beau said. I'm sorry. "I have to go. My job starts tonight. *Je t'aime. Au revoir."* He ended the call before his mother could get all wound up and talk for another thirty minutes.

Beau didn't have time to talk. He'd been hired by Senator Marcus Anderson to protect his daughter Aurelie.

Miss Anderson had received a number of death threats over the past week since the senator had announced his reelection campaign. At the same time, Aurelie had stepped in to lead her father's philanthropic effort to preserve the bayou.

Since the senator would be campaigning across the state, he wouldn't have time to be with his daughter to guarantee her safety.

That would be Beau's responsibility.

The senator didn't want his daughter to know he'd hired a bodyguard. At least, not yet. He'd warned Beau that his daughter could be headstrong and extremely stubborn, a trait she'd inherited from her father.

Great. Beau wasn't thrilled with the idea of babysitting a spoiled little rich girl with a rebellious streak. He'd have to be on his toes at all times to make certain she didn't ghost him and land herself in trouble with no one around to help.

What she probably needed was a good old-fashioned spanking to get her attention. He'd almost asked the senator if that was a possibility but had thought better of it.

This was his first assignment with the Brotherhood Protectors. He wanted it to be a success and good advertisement for future gigs. Word of mouth was the best kind of marketing in the security business.

He pulled on the green cloth mask he'd acquired with the costume, thinking it appropriate for this undercover bodyguard job.

The event at the Gautreaux Chateau was a masquerade ball to raise money for the senator's reelection campaign. Only the very wealthy had purchased tickets at ten thousand dollars each.

Beau wouldn't be going to the event if the Senator hadn't given him a free ticket. He'd have been standing guard at the door or pacing the perimeter.

Ten-thousand-dollar tickets?

No way.

He had the money, but he had other plans for his savings—a place of his own with a house and five to ten acres of good land where he could raise a garden, a cow or two, and chickens. If it was on the bayou...even better. He'd always wanted a boat dock and access to fishing whenever he had a spare moment.

His mother had offered to give each of her children ten acres out of the one hundred and twenty acres that had been in their family for over two hundred years. So far, only two of her ten children had taken her up on that offer.

As much as Beau loved his mother, he couldn't see living that close. As it was, being in the same parish was almost too close. He was always running into those of his siblings who hadn't left Bayou Mambaloa to find employment in the bigger cities, like New Orleans or Baton Rouge.

No. He wanted to purchase his own property, preferably on the other side of the parish, with a little distance between them to discourage his mother from "dropping in" whenever she felt like it.

Oh, he loved his mother, but he also loved his privacy. As a widow with no husband to occupy her time, Josephine Boyette took her mothering to the extreme, trying to solve every problem for every one of her children instead of letting them figure it out on their own.

He'd limited his time with her since he'd been back, afraid she'd dig into his problems and find out he wasn't as okay as he'd led her to believe.

He'd been working through his issues with the therapist the VA hospital had assigned since he'd returned from his last mission with the Army Rangers.

As the sole survivor of a helicopter crash, he'd been so messed up he hadn't wanted to get out of bed for a month. That and the broken leg hadn't helped.

But that was in the past. He'd been through hundreds of hours of physical and mental therapy and was more than ready to get on with his life.

His teammates who'd perished in the crash couldn't get on with their lives, and they'd never know the wonderful trouble of being psychoanalyzed by their mothers.

How many times had he been told he was the lucky one?

And why didn't he feel lucky?

A weight threatened to settle on his chest, pushing out the air he'd been breathing.

Now was not the time to backslide into the black funk he'd clawed his way out of over six months ago.

Beau pushed open the door of his truck and dropped to the ground. He squared his shoulders and marched toward the entrance, careful not to limp on the leg that would never be the same.

He was determined to do his best to help the senator, make a good impression for the Bayou Brotherhood Protectors and keep Miss Anderson safe.

A man in a black suit stood guard at the door, checking IDs and tickets of each guest as they arrived.

Out of his element at such a formal function, Beau adjusted his Robin Hood hat. When the guard asked for his ID, he presented his military ID, his ten-thousand-dollar ticket and raised his mask briefly.

Beau entered the 18th-century mansion and was immediately struck by the opulent marble flooring and the double sweeping staircases on each side of the foyer, rising to the second level. A man dressed in a livery suit held out his hands. "May I take your... jacket...or quiver of arrows?"

"No, thank you," Beau said. "But perhaps you can tell me where I can find Senator Anderson."

"The senator is in the ballroom receiving line," the servant said and waved an arm toward the sound of music coming from a wide-open doorway.

Beau crossed the marble floor and entered a large ballroom crowded with people in a variety of costumes.

A man wearing an Abraham Lincoln outfit stood just inside the doorway, greeting guests as they entered.

Abraham Lincoln held out his hand. "Welcome to the Harlequins and Heartthrobs Masquerade Ball and reelection campaign fundraiser. Thank you for your support."

Beau gripped the man's hand. "I assume you're Senator Anderson," he said.

The man dressed as Abraham Lincoln smiled. "Your assumption is correct. And to whom do I have the pleasure of speaking?"

Beau dipped his head. "I'm Beau Boyette, an agent

of the Brotherhood Protectors. I was sent to help you with your situation."

The senator's smile faded, and his grip tightened on Beau's hand. "Thank you for coming so quickly."

Beau's glance swept the ballroom. "Is the object of your concern here tonight?"

The man with the Abraham Lincoln top hat and black jacket gave a brief nod. "She is."

Beau looked around the ballroom again. "Will you introduce me to her to get the ball rolling?"

Abraham shook his head. "My daughter is a strong-minded, independent woman. She won't be happy that I've hired somebody to protect her. For now, I'd rather let you acquaint yourself with her. If that doesn't work, I'll introduce you as a son of a friend of mine."

Beau nodded. "As you wish. At the very least, could you point her out to me?"

The senator glanced around the ballroom. "She's dressed as Amelia Earhart, in trousers, a dusty-brown jacket and goggles instead of a mask." The man shook his head. "I couldn't get her to wear a dress to save my life."

Beau's lips twitched. "She sounds like she has a mind of her own."

The senator chuckled. "That she does." He lifted his chin, indicating direction. "That's her dancing with my executive assistant. At least the ballroom dance lessons that I paid for weren't wasted. They would've looked better if she were wearing the antebellum dress I had commissioned for her."

The woman in the goggles waltzed past Beau in the arms of a man dressed as a swashbuckling pirate.

Now, that was a costume. Beau wished he'd had more time to find a better disguise than the Robin Hood one, which was the last decent choice at the costume shop in New Orleans.

He hadn't had time to go to a different costume shop, given that he'd only been notified of this mission around noon that day. His only other choice was a hairy Sasquatch costume.

Although, he was now beginning to wish he'd gone with Sasquatch. He felt very exposed wearing green tights, even though the jacket was long enough, just barely covering his ass.

"Good luck keeping up with her," the senator said.

Beau's lips pressed together as he watched the woman laugh out loud at something the pirate said. "I'll take it from here," he said, leaving the senator at his post receiving guests.

Beau wandered into the ballroom, his gaze on Amelia Earhart, a.k.a. Aurelie Anderson. He stopped at a table serving lemonade and what appeared to be mint juleps. He chose a lemonade and stood back, watching Miss Anderson dance around the room with the pirate. As he sipped the lemonade, he thought through the different scenarios where he could introduce himself.

The woman appeared relaxed, dancing and talking with the senator's executive assistant. Her movements appeared effortless, a testimony to the dance lessons her father had paid for her to take. An orchestra provided the music, playing various reimagined modern songs in an 18th-century style.

As the song came to a close, Miss Anderson and her partner slowed to stop. The pirate gave her a sweeping bow and then waved a hand toward the open bar.

Aurelie shook her head and said something Beau couldn't hear. Then, she walked away from the executive assistant. She ducked through a doorway and disappeared.

Beau set his glass down on an empty tray and hurried to follow. He left through the same door that she had and walked quickly down a hallway. He spotted her pushing through another doorway further down the corridor.

Though he hurried to catch up, he came to an abrupt halt in front of the swinging door with a placard indicating that the room inside was the ladies' restroom.

Since he couldn't follow her through that door, he walked further down the hall and stood in front of the men's room, waiting for Miss Anderson to emerge.

A few minutes later, the senator's daughter emerged from the bathroom.

When she looked in his direction, Beau pretended to be coming out of the men's room. She only gave him a cursory glance before she headed back to the ballroom, her shoulders back, head held high as if she were marching into battle.

Beau followed and found her standing against the wall, her foot tapping to the beat of the music. Beau crossed to the lemonade table, snagged two glasses of lemonade and walked back to where Miss Anderson stood half-hidden by a potted plant. He stopped next to her without looking at her, his gaze on the people dancing across the floor. Eventually, he held up the glass to her. "You look like you need this more than I do."

She took the glass from him and downed most of it in one long swallow. "Thanks, I did need that."

He chuckled. "Do you always dance so rigorously?"

She lifted her chin. "A wise person once told me to put your heart and soul into everything you do, or don't bother doing it at all."

"Have you ever bothered to do the nothing at all?" He quirked his lips upward on the corners in challenge.

"A number of times," the Anderson woman said.

"Now that you've consumed an entire glass of lemonade given to you by a complete stranger, did you stop to think I might have spiked that lemonade with a date rape drug?" he asked.

Her brow wrinkled. "You don't look like the type of man who would spike a girl's drink."

He looked down at his costume. "Is it the costume?"

She laughed. "Partly. And the fact that you wouldn't have given me the lemonade spiked with any drug with my father watching like a hawk." She lifted her chin toward the man dressed as Abraham Lincoln. "He's been watching me all evening. He even enlisted his executive assistant to have a pity-dance with me to keep me busy."

"I'm sure your father's assistant didn't consider dancing with you in any way pitiful." Beau tipped his head toward the couples dancing to the music. "You held your own on the dance floor."

Aurelie met his gaze. "You were watching that long?"

"I was," he admitted.

"That's kind of creepy," she commented. "I might reconsider my earlier opinion about you." She touched a hand to her throat. "Perhaps you did spike my lemonade."

Beau's lips twitched. "I didn't, but I can under-stand President Lincoln's concern for his daughter," he said. "Considering the fact he was assassinated, he has good reason to be a little paranoid."

Her lips curved into a smile, transforming her face and making it softer and more approachable.

"You have a point." She held out her hand. "I'm Amelia Earhart. Nice to meet you."

So, she was going to play it that way. "Robin Hood," he said as he took her hand.

Her grip was firm, not limp like many of the women with whom Beau had shaken hands.

"Robin Hood, you say?" Aurelie cocked an eyebrow in challenge. "I had pegged you as Peter Pan."

He released her hand and pressed his over his heart. "You wound me, madame." Beau shook his head. "I would think my quiver of arrows and the bow would have given it away."

She chuckled. "They are quite impressive. How about those tights? Should I assume anything about your sexuality?"

His hand remaining on his chest, Beau shook his head. "Again, you wound me, madame. I assure you I'm more attracted to Maid Marian than Friar Tuck."

Miss Anderson chuckled. "For what it's worth, the tights look good on you."

He dipped his head. "I'll take that as a compliment."

"As you should." She glanced around the room. "Now, if you'll excuse me, I'm working."

"Working?" he lifted both eyebrows.

Still looking around the room, she answered, "This is a fundraiser. My job is to make sure the guests are happy."

Beau nodded. "And happy guests mean more contributions to President Lincoln's reelection campaign, right?"

Her brow wrinkled. "Of course."

"Then, perhaps, you might consider entertaining this guest with a dance?"

Her lips twisted. "Sir, I believe you're quite capable of entertaining yourself." She started to walk away.

"Then perhaps, you might consider taking pity on a man in tights who is sure to be avoided by every available female in the ballroom and dance with me. I would consider it an honor," he performed a deep bow, "and a heroic way to help me salvage my eligible bachelor status."

She shook her head. "More likely salvaging your ego. Although, I doubt you'll lack a partner. Many of the matrons will be vying for you to join them in a dance."

"Only if I first prove I can dance."

Aurelie canted her head to one side, her gaze raking over him. "True. Not many men can dance. Or, truthfully, *like* to dance."

"I can and do like to dance. My mother made certain all her boys could represent the family properly on the dance floor."

"Forced to take lessons?" She shook her head. "Me, too."

"More like forced to learn." Beau hadn't always

appreciated having to learn to dance with his mother and sisters as his partners. Not until he'd grown older and interested in girls had he understood the value. The ladies usually loved to dance, and most of his male friends didn't or wouldn't. "My mother was a very good teacher. She and my father loved to dance at festivals and parties."

She drew in a deep breath and let it out. "In the spirit of showing the other women in attendance that you can and will dance, I suppose I could spare a pity dance with the man in green tights." She held out her hand. "Come on, Peter Pan. Let's show them what you've got."

"Robin Hood," he corrected as he took her hand and led her out into the middle of the ballroom as the orchestra began a new song.

After the first three notes, Beau recognized the song as "Can't Help Falling In Love," made famous by the late crooner Elvis Presley.

"Good grief," Aurelie murmured.

"It's a sign," Beau said as he glided across the floor, super glad his mother had insisted on him learning to waltz.

Aurelie needed little guidance to execute the dance. She usually had to lead when her male partners couldn't. With Peter Pan, she played a little push-me-pull-me until she finally let him take control. "You say your mother taught you to dance?"

He nodded. "She insisted on us learning to be as

fluid and graceful as Fred Astaire." Beau grinned. "She loved all his movies, especially those when he partnered with Ginger Rogers."

"Let me guess..." Aurelie said, "she made you watch the movies as well?"

He nodded.

"And your father had no say in the matter?"

"None," Beau said. "When it came to our education, both in school and on the dance floor, he let her take the lead."

"A hands-off father?" She snorted softly. "What's that like?"

"Oh, he wasn't a hands-off father; he just knew which battles to choose. He taught us other things."

"Like?" She prompted.

"How to open doors for women, the elderly, and...well, anyone." He grinned. "He taught all of us about the bayou, to include frog gigging, how to spot alligators, shrimping, crabbing, fishing, cleaning and preparing the food we caught. He also taught us about vehicle maintenance like changing oil, tires and spark plugs."

"Even your sisters?" Aurelie asked.

Beau nodded. "Absolutely. Our mother could do all those things; she just preferred not to. Before all of us kids, she helped him on his fishing boat. Even after we came along, she still loved fishing with my father."

Aurelie frowned. "How many children did your mother and father have?"

"There are ten of us," Beau said and waited for the shock on her pretty face. He wasn't disappointed.

"Ten?" Her feet faltered.

Beau's arms tightened around her, and he effortlessly swung her out and back into his arms. "That's right. They had ten children."

"That's a lot of mouths to feed," Aurelie frowned. "Wow."

He laughed. "My grandparents considered my father an underachiever."

Her frown deepened. "Why?"

"His brother sired nineteen children. My father didn't even come close."

Aurelie's brow furrowed. "You're not serious, are you?"

"As serious as the heart attack that claimed my uncle's life when the youngest set of twins was only five years old," Beau said, his voice growing soft. He'd been in Iraq when his uncle had passed. His father had done his best to help the family out. Fortunately, his brother had been a shrewd investor and had taken out a sizable life insurance policy when he'd been younger. After selling the family boat-building business, his aunt had managed the investments and the houseful of children like the CEO of a major corporation.

"Youngest set of twins?" the woman in his arms asked.

"That's right," he said. "I think there are three or four sets of twins." Beau twirled her away and back into his arms. "Does that bother you that I'm from a family of many children?"

"No, why should it?"

"Do you even like children?" he asked.

She blinked. "Of course I do."

"Do you have any siblings?" he asked, though he already knew the answer.

Aurelie shook her head. "I always wished I had a brother or sister. You're fortunate to have some."

His lips twisted into a wry grin. "Others might not think so. There's never a moment's peace when we're all together."

"I hope to have children someday. Not just one child. I don't wish that on anyone. It can be very lonely."

"And quiet," Beau said with a sigh.

She laughed. "I take it you value silence."

"I do," he said. "But I love my brothers and sisters very much, even though they can drive me crazy at times."

The five-string quartet transitioned into another song, not a waltz, but one that allowed Beau to slow to a rocking motion. His arm circled the small of her back, and he pulled her closer. "Speaking of silence..."

He rested his cheek against her temple. "You smell good."

"What does that have to do with silence?" she asked, her body stiff.

"Nothing. But if we don't talk, we can almost imagine Elvis singing this one."

She moved in rhythm with him to the orchestra's version of "Love Me Tender."

Together, they fit perfectly, a fact that gave Beau pause. The more he held her, the more he wanted to.

Dangerous...dangerous thoughts.

Yet, he didn't relinquish his hold.

Slowly, her body melted into his. As the song came to its beautiful end, Beau dipped Aurelie low in his arms and kissed her.

As their lips met, the music ended.

She opened to him, letting him in for a brief and delicious taste. For a moment, their tongues touched and caressed. For a moment, he forgot where he was and that he was on a mission to protect this woman, not make out with her in front of her father and the rich and influential people there to contribute to the senator's campaign.

When he brought her back up, he stared into her goggles, wishing he could see her eyes. He wondered what color they were, what they would tell him and if she'd enjoyed the dance and the kiss as much as he had.

He might not be able to see her eyes, but he could

feel the change in her body where his hands still rested against her back.

Aurelie stiffened. "Excuse me."

She stepped backward, spun on her booted heels and darted for the hallway where the bathrooms were located.

Beau started to follow.

"What the hell was that?" a voice said behind him in a tight whisper.

He turned to face an angry Abe Lincoln.

"I introduced myself to your daughter." He couldn't have come up with a dumber response if he'd tried. But once it left his lips, he couldn't take it back.

"And that gives you leave to grope her on the dance floor? What kind of operation is this Brotherhood Protectors?"

Fuck.

He'd blown it with the man who'd hired him. What had he been thinking, kissing the man's daughter?

"My apologies, sir. It must have been the song." Beau glanced toward the hallway where Aurelie had gone. "If you'll excuse me, I need to follow her and make sure she's all right."

"Damn right, you do. And while you're at it, try not to molest her." As he turned away, he muttered, "What's wrong with the young people today?"

Beau didn't try to answer the man. He strode out

of the ballroom into the corridor. This time, he didn't see Aurelie walking into the bathroom. She was nowhere to be seen, as if she'd disappeared.

With the kiss still fresh on his lips, he ran to the ladies' room door and knocked on the contoured panel.

An older woman dressed as the Queen of Hearts pulled the door open.

Beau frowned. "Did you see Miss..." he thought better of asking if the woman had seen Miss Anderson and amended, "Amelia Earhart?"

The woman shook her head. "I was the only person in here." She stepped out of the bathroom, her gaze sweeping him from top to toe. "Let me know if you can't find her. I'm available all night." With a wink, she walked away.

Holy shit.

His first day on the job, and he'd already lost the client.

ABOUT THE AUTHOR

ELLE JAMES also writing as MYLA JACKSON is a *New York Times* and *USA Today* Bestselling author of books including cowboys, intrigues and paranormal adventures that keep her readers on the edges of their seats. When she's not at her computer, she's traveling, snow skiing, boating, or riding her ATV, dreaming up new stories. Learn more about Elle James at www.ellejames.com

Website | Facebook | Twitter | GoodReads |
Newsletter | BookBub | Amazon

Or visit her alter ego Myla Jackson at
mylajackson.com
Website | Facebook | Twitter | Newsletter

Follow Me!
www.ellejames.com
ellejamesauthor@gmail.com

ALSO BY ELLE JAMES

Gerard (#2)

Lucas (#3)

Beau (#4)

Rafael (#5)

Valentin (#6)

Landry (#7)

Simon (#8)

Maurice (#9)

Jacques (#10)

Brotherhood Protectors Yellowstone

Saving Kyla (#1)

Saving Chelsea (#2)

Saving Amanda (#3)

Saving Liliana (#4)

Saving Breely (#5)

Saving Savvie (#6)

Saving Jenna (#7)

Saving Peyton (#8)

Saving Londyn (#9)

Brotherhood Protectors Colorado

SEAL Salvation (#1)

Rocky Mountain Rescue (#2)

Ranger Redemption (#3)

Tactical Takeover (#4)

Colorado Conspiracy (#5)

Rocky Mountain Madness (#6)

Free Fall (#7)

Colorado Cold Case (#8)

Fool's Folly (#9)

Colorado Free Rein (#10)

Rocky Mountain Venom (#11)

High Country Hero (#12)

Brotherhood Protectors

Montana SEAL (#1)

Bride Protector SEAL (#2)

Montana D-Force (#3)

Cowboy D-Force (#4)

Montana Ranger (#5)

Montana Dog Soldier (#6)

Montana SEAL Daddy (#7)

Montana Ranger's Wedding Vow (#8)

Montana SEAL Undercover Daddy (#9)

Cape Cod SEAL Rescue (#10)

Montana SEAL Friendly Fire (#11)

Montana SEAL's Mail-Order Bride (#12)

SEAL Justice (#13)

Ranger Creed (#14)

Delta Force Rescue (#15)

Dog Days of Christmas (#16)

Montana Rescue (#17)

Montana Ranger Returns (#18)

Brotherhood Protectors Boxed Set 1

Brotherhood Protectors Boxed Set 2

Brotherhood Protectors Boxed Set 3

Brotherhood Protectors Boxed Set 4

Brotherhood Protectors Boxed Set 5

Brotherhood Protectors Boxed Set 6

Iron Horse Legacy

Soldier's Duty (#1)

Ranger's Baby (#2)

Marine's Promise (#3)

SEAL's Vow (#4)

Warrior's Resolve (#5)

Drake (#6)

Grimm (#7)

Murdock (#8)

Utah (#9)

Judge (#10)

Delta Force Strong

Ivy's Delta (Delta Force 3 Crossover)

Breaking Silence (#1)

Breaking Rules (#2)

Breaking Away (#3)

Breaking Free (#4)

Breaking Hearts (#5)

Breaking Ties (#6)

Breaking Point (#7)

Breaking Dawn (#8)

Breaking Promises (#9)

Hearts & Heroes Series

Wyatt's War (#1)

Mack's Witness (#2)

Ronin's Return (#3)

Sam's Surrender (#4)

Hellfire Series

Hellfire, Texas (#1)

Justice Burning (#2)

Smoldering Desire (#3)

Hellfire in High Heels (#4)

Playing With Fire (#5)

Up in Flames (#6)

Total Meltdown (#7)

Take No Prisoners Series

The Billionaire Replacement Date (#8) coming soon

The Billionaire Wedding Date (#9) coming soon

Cajun Magic Mystery Series

Voodoo on the Bayou (#1)

Voodoo for Two (#2)

Deja Voodoo (#3)

Cajun Magic Mysteries Books 1-3

The Outriders

Homicide at Whiskey Gulch (#1)

Hideout at Whiskey Gulch (#2)

Held Hostage at Whiskey Gulch (#3)

Setup at Whiskey Gulch (#4)

Missing Witness at Whiskey Gulch (#5)

Cowboy Justice at Whiskey Gulch (#6)

Boys Behaving Badly Anthologies

Rogues (#1)

Blue Collar (#2)

Pirates (#3)

Stranded (#4)

First Responder (#5)

Silver Soldier's (#6)

Warrior's Conquest

Enslaved by the Viking Short Story

Conquests

Smokin' Hot Firemen

Protecting the Colton Bride

Protecting the Colton Bride & Colton's Cowboy Code

Heir to Murder

Secret Service Rescue

High Octane Heroes

Haunted

Engaged with the Boss

Cowboy Brigade

An Unexpected Clue

Under Suspicion, With Child

Texas-Size Secrets

Made in the USA
Monee, IL
28 December 2024

75604266R00164